To Alzada. Thanks so much!

Life is But a Dream

A NOVEL

Jennifer Provenza

Calabria Press

ISBN-13:9780692675335
ISBN-10:0692675337
Library of Congress Control Number: 2016905239
Calabria Press, Sacramento, CA

Cover design by Ian Wallace
Author photo by Kristin Hoebermann

For Ian, my love. And for May and Clara: I loved you before I met you.

Chapter I

I WAS THREE years old the first time it happened. Or, more accurately I suppose, it was the first time I remember it happening. I had a babysitter that night, and my mother had promised me that if she received a good report from the teenage girl who had been hired to watch me for a few hours, I would be allowed to have a piece of special candy she kept hidden in her top dresser drawer. I had behaved perfectly all evening, had eaten all my dinner, drawn a picture for my parents, and even brushed my teeth without complaining. So when I heard my parents' car enter the driveway, I jumped out of bed and tore down the stairs, my little bare feet tapping on the hardwood floor. I wore my favorite nightgown; my teddy bear had a matching miniature version. I clutched him tightly to my chest as I ran. My father opened the door. He looked older, even then, more like my grandpa than my father, with his gray beard and spectacles low on his nose. But despite his age, he crouched down and opened his arms to me, and I ran at him, crashing into his hug and knocking him backward against the door.

"I was good, Daddy!" I said.

He glanced up at the babysitter, and she nodded.

"Okay, then," he said, "you can go up and get your candy."

I licked my lips, turned around, and made a run for it up the stairs. And then it happened. All of a sudden, the stairs, solidly beneath my feet a moment ago, were gone. My mommy and daddy were gone. The babysitter was gone. And I was…I was somewhere else. I was in a comfortable bed in a dark room. And on my chest was a puppy, licking my nose.

And somehow, at that moment, I knew that the puppy was named Chester and that my mom had brought him home from the shelter that morning. But why was I in bed when I had just been on the stairs?

"Mommy!"

In a moment, my mother was in the room.

"Chester, no! Leave Angie alone, silly puppy." She picked him up, and he licked her on the cheek. She stroked his golden fur.

"Mommy, I want my candy," I said. "I was good for the babysitter."

My mom smiled at me. "I think someone was having a dream. You didn't have a babysitter tonight. Remember, we all watched Charlie Brown and then carved the pumpkin."

Something was very wrong. I knew that, just a few moments ago, I had been running up the stairs to get my candy, and now I was in bed.

"What's a dream?" I said.

"It's okay, baby. Sometimes dreams seem very real."

I stuck out my lower lip. "I don't dream. I just go to my other house."

My mom shook her head, kissed my nose, and left the room. I yawned and closed my eyes.

And then I was back on the stairs. But something was wrong. Something was very, very wrong. I was lying on the stairs, and my mother was cradling my head. There was searing pain shooting through my mouth, and a pool of red liquid was all around us. I began to cry, tears mingling with the blood on the stairs.

"Oh, thank God you're awake. Honey, she's awake. Sweetheart, you fell on the stairs, and you hit your chin. I think you bit through your tongue," my mom said.

I tried to talk, but I couldn't get my tongue to move right. I gurgled.

"Oh God, okay, let's get her in the car. Did you get through to the doctor yet?"

I heard my parents talking. We were going to the doctor. I wondered what he would do. Would he put a Band-Aid on my tongue? Could he stitch it up? I didn't want a needle in my tongue.

In the end the doctor didn't do anything but give me some pain medicine. The next memory I had was of my mother tucking me into bed hours later.

"I didn't fall," I said.

"What?"

I looked closer at my mom. Why was her hair light brown? I could have sworn it was blond when she came in to take Chester away.

"I didn't fall. Chester just woke me up."

"Who's Chester?"

"My puppy. In my other house. The one we live in sometimes."

She wrinkled her brow. "Angie, you were unconscious for a few minutes. Unconscious means asleep. I think maybe you were dreaming while you were asleep."

"No! It wasn't a dream. It was real."

"Okay," she said. Then she stroked my hair and turned off the ballerina lamp beside my bed. "Sweet dreams."

Chapter 2

Friday, July 8, 1:36 a.m., New York

I AM AT The Drunken Horse with my friends from graduate school, seated next to the fireplace. It is the first time that all of us have gotten together since graduation two years ago, and it took Meredith's bachelorette party to get us here.

I feel flushed. My vodka martini is warm in my chest, and my cheeks are hot in the glow of the fire.

Meredith holds up her glass. "Here's to my last night of freedom! And my last night of drinking...Mark wants to start trying for a baby on the honeymoon."

"Well, you'll be a natural at motherhood," I say. "And don't worry. It seems scary at first, but you figure it out."

"How do you know?" My friend Jana laughs.

I feel my cheeks burn even hotter. "I...used to babysit a lot."

"Yeah, okay," Meredith says, "I'm sure that's exactly the same."

By the time I leave The Drunken Horse, I've finished three martinis, which is two more than my body can really handle. Luckily, I'm not far from home. I clutch Jana's hand as we stumble down the street. My silver heels dig into my toes, and I walk faster. In the distance, I can see the Empire State Building lit up against the night sky. Tonight, it's blue.

"I love New York!"

"Of course you do," Jana says. "It's the best city on earth."

Jana leaves me at my door and hails a cab. Somehow, I make it upstairs and manage to get myself into a nightshirt and under the covers before I pass out.

Saturday, July 9, 10:58 a.m., Sacramento

I feel the sun on my eyelids before I open my eyes.

"Morning, Angie," I hear. "We slept late, cutie. It's almost eleven."

Of course. I was out late at that party in New York, I think. But I don't say it. I wish I could remember what exactly the party was for, but the details are hazy. I know I was with Meredith and everyone from grad school. Sometimes I clearly remember the day before in my other life, but other times it's a bit cloudy.

I nestle into the crisp white cotton sheets and pull the fluffy white duvet closer around me. Wedding gifts. Four years later they still feel new and special. I push my body up against my husband. He pulls me to him and hugs me tight.

"You smell good," I say.

He laughs. "Really? Not like I need to take a shower?"

I giggle and bite my lip. "No." I kiss him.

"I dreamed about you," he whispers, holding me close.

I've always wondered what it must be like to dream. To close my eyes and drift peacefully into a temporary oblivion. Perhaps it would feel like floating on a cloud, images passing before my eyes like genial hallucinations. Maybe it would feel more like being underwater, the world looking just a bit out of focus and surreal. My brother used to tell me about lucid dreams, the kind where he knew he was dreaming. It would happen sometimes when he was having a nightmare, and then, all of a sudden, just as he was about to be stabbed or eaten or whatever, he would realize it was just a dream and say to himself, *Open your eyes*, and he would, just like that.

I playfully start to tickle Steve, but the door creaks open.

I know without even looking that it's Ella. "Morning, Ell. Sorry we slept so late."

Ella jumps up onto the bed, burrowing under the covers and between her father and me as though she were a little puppy. I kiss her chubby little cheek. At three years old, she still has some baby fat and some darling little curls in her light brown hair. When she was a baby, Steve nicknamed her Chubby McButter Pants because she was so fat. I love those little rolls on her legs.

"Are you hungry, honey?"

She raises one eyebrow. "No. I got me breakfast."

"You got breakfast all by yourself?" I'm beginning to regret getting up so late. "What did you eat?"

"Cheerios!"

I squeeze my lips into a forced smile. "Good job, baby."

Steve ruffles her hair and asks her if she wants to watch cartoons, while I head out into the kitchen to survey the damage.

It's not as bad as I feared. The box of Cheerios is lying on the floor, much of its contents on the beige carpet. Luckily, Ella didn't get to the milk in the fridge, so all I have to do is vacuum up the cereal.

As I vacuum, Steve sits on the couch with Ella on his lap and reaches for the remote. Soon the room is filled with the overwhelmingly loud sound of cartoon theme songs.

"Honey, please!" I shout over the vacuum.

"What—she can't hear it with that noise."

I let it go. I love watching Steve with Ella.

The rest of the day passes quietly. After showering, we dress Ella in a white tank top and shorts. She insists on wearing her ballet tutu to complete the ensemble, and once we manage to hook her into the car seat, still in her tutu, we head to Bel Air Market. As usual, Ella is her vivacious self, calling out hello to everyone she sees.

That night, we watch a movie (*Chitty Chitty Bang Bang*), eat some leftover pizza for dinner, and carry Ella to bed after she falls asleep on the couch. She looks beautiful with her eyes closed, so peaceful. I wonder what she dreams. No matter how hard I try to imagine dreaming, I feel like a blind person trying to grasp the idea of colors. Because I've never had a dream in my life, at least not the way normal people have dreams. As far as I know, I've never even really slept. My life just continuously goes, with no rest. Both of my lives do actually.

In bed with Steve, I snuggle under his arm into my "spot." It is only eight o'clock, but Steve has adjusted to my need to be in bed early. I can afford to go to bed a bit later in New York. But here, I really have to turn in early if I don't want to sleep the day away in Manhattan. We kiss, and he feels so solid, so alive. I know this moment is real; this moment has to be real. I'll miss Steve tomorrow. And Ella. But the time will pass quickly, I'm sure.

Chapter 3

Saturday, July 9, 11:00 a.m., New York

I awaken a split second later in my bed in my apartment. My head feels like someone is hacking at it with an ax, my bladder is about to overflow, and I feel vaguely like I might need to vomit. Wonderful. My hangover, interrupted by my sojourn to California, has finally caught up with me.

I sit up in my tiny bed and wince. Actually, it's a double bed, but it feels tiny compared to my California king-sized bed back in Sacramento. The full is all I can fit in my shoe box of a bedroom, however. Not that the apartment comes cheap. I pay $2,000 a month for my tiny studio in Chelsea (complete with leaks, cockroaches, and the occasional mouse) and consider it a good deal. I feel sticky all over, the July humidity seeping through the sheets. I sit up in bed and pull my hair up into a bun. Then I grab my hair clip from the nightstand and secure the bun on my head. I prefer the dry heat of the Sacramento valley. It's especially hard for me because I can never fully get used to the weather in one place.

I stand up and then break into a sprint as a wave of nausea runs over me. Luckily, I make it to the toilet on time. After getting sick, I stand and glance at myself in the mirror. I am briefly surprised to see my hair ending before it reaches my shoulders—I wear it longer in California. Otherwise, I look exactly the same as I do in my other life.

I turn on the cold-water tap of my tiny little sink and then wash my face. The crumbling blue-and-white tile feels pleasantly cool under my feet. I grab a towel from the back of the door and dry my face as I walk toward the window to switch on the air conditioner. The lights dim as it lurches on, spewing some dust into the air and making a loud humming noise. The only view out the window is the alley behind the building. Sometimes little kids bounce a ball back there and hit it against my window, startling me.

Ella would probably love to play back there. But I would never let her; it's far too dirty.

Shaking my head, I peel off my damp nightshirt and head back into the bathroom.

After my shower, I throw on some clothes, take two ibuprofen tablets with a sip of water, and then rush out of the house to meet my mom for brunch at French Roast. I start out at a brisk walk, but after the second block I have to slow down because of the heat and the pounding in my head. After what feels like more than five blocks, I reach the restaurant and step through the door. A cool blast of air hits me as I enter. My mom is already seated and drinking an iced tea. She looks cool and collected, as usual, her perfectly French-manicured nails tapping the table as she waits. Her dyed-blond hair somehow manages to hold its shape, despite the heat, and her skin looks smooth and soft. I wave and bypass the hostess, plopping into the seat across from my mother.

"Hi, honey!" she says, reaching across the table and squeezing my hand. "I love your outfit. That skirt looks cute with that striped top. I just love the clothes this season. They're so French!"

I smile. "Thanks. I feel kind of like a wilted flower at the moment."

"Well, you don't look like one. Did you go shopping without me?"

"I went to Express just to browse yesterday, and I ended up spending two hundred bucks."

Mom laughs. "Yeah, you should have seen me last week at Bloomingdale's. I bought three of the same purse, in different colors. I would have bought some pants, but I'm too fat. It's just depressing."

"Mom, you're not fat." My mother has never weighed more than 115 pounds in her life.

"Well, I'm going on a diet. It's just so frustrating. But I'm not breaking down and buying a size four again."

"It's probably just one of those weird hormonal fluctuations, Mom."

"I don't get my period anymore. I just shouldn't eat anything. Do you want to share something?"

"No, thanks. You know how I am. I'll just be eating a second breakfast in an hour if I don't eat enough now."

She smiles. "Well, you don't need to worry about your weight. That's fine. I'll just have some yogurt. Ooh, you know what you should get? The goat-cheese omelet with sausage. Then I can have a bite."

"Sure, Mom."

By the time the food arrives, I'm famished. I take a bite of my omelet, and it's perfect: soft eggs; melted, rich goat cheese; and hot, juicy sausage. The texture, the taste, it is all perfectly real. I just can't believe that a dream experience could be so concrete. And then there is the restaurant. The mirrored wall with the French bistro entrées scrawled in pastel green. The mahogany bar, the tables crammed together, the men drinking coffee and laughing, the woman spooning fruit into her child's mouth. All of these things are so solidly before me, yet Steve would have me believe this whole experience is a dream. Just as everyone here believes Steve doesn't exist.

At least I don't have to worry that my mom doesn't exist at all, because she, my dad, and my older brother, Jonathan, are part of both of my lives.

"So, how's *Medea* coming, honey?" my mom says.

"Pretty good." I dip my fork into her plate and stab a yogurt-covered strawberry. "My design's coming along. The director decided to set the play in Nazi Germany, so I'm trying to play with the idea that Medea is this outsider. I'm going to dress her like a Gypsy, in these flowing skirts and stuff. I'll show you my sketches. They're really cool. I'm doing them with oil pastels on black paper."

"I can't wait to see them! You always design such beautiful costumes." My mom takes a bite of my omelet and makes a face. She always forgets that she doesn't like goat cheese. "Why don't you ever get to keep them?"

"Because that just isn't how it works. But I get to keep my sketches."

"Those are works of art in and of themselves. Soon you'll be designing for Broadway."

"Thanks. I appreciate your confidence, but that's probably a little ways away. What's Dad doing this morning?" I ask.

"Oh, he's tinkering with his models. Like usual."

The rest of the day is spent working on my sketch of Medea's children, although I take a break to check my e-mail and eat a peanut butter and jelly sandwich. Tomorrow I have to get up early because Steve and Ella and I are going to Lake Tahoe for the day. So at only nine o'clock, I climb into bed and turn out the light, knowing that as soon as I fall asleep, I will instantly awaken—and it will be twelve hours later (except because of the time change between California and New York, it will actually only be 6:00 a.m.), and I'll be in California with Steve and Ella. I wonder if there is anyone else out there like me. Suddenly, I feel overwhelmingly tired, and the next thing I know, it is morning.

Monday, July 18, 4:30 p.m., New York

I take a sip of my Diet Coke and scan the director's face, looking for some sign of a reaction. We are having a production meeting for a new version of *Medea*. This is my first time working for the Atlantic Theater Company, a highly respected Off Broadway theater. If my work goes over well, this could open up a lot of doors for me. Especially because I'm not part of the Yale "mafia," the circle of designers who graduated from Yale and whose fellow alumni make sure they get lots of plum jobs. Of course, having come from NYU's graduate design program, I'm still in a pretty good position. I tap my foot on the stained linoleum, waiting for a response.

Finally, Lynne Clemens, the director, glances up at me.

"Okay, now tell me why you have the children dressed in folk costume here." Her voice is powerful, as is her presence. She is very well known and respected in the New York theater world.

I am confident in my design. I take a deep breath.

"Well, I think it is important that the children look very German in this scene, to show how their father has taken them fully into his world and separated them from Medea and from her foreignness."

The director nods her head vigorously. She opens her mouth to speak, but before the words leave her lips, my head falls forward as I am rendered unconscious.

Tuesday, July 19, 1:30 a.m., Sacramento

I am in my bed in California. Steve is beside me. Piercing screams are coming from Ella's room.

"Steve, this cannot be happening. Not now." *Not now.* Any other time today, it could have been okay. But no, now, right now, in the middle of my production meeting, Ella is having one of her night terrors.

I shake my husband. "Steve, take care of this, please!" Then grabbing my earplugs from the nightstand and stuffing them in my ears, I turn over onto my stomach and try to fall asleep.

Monday, July 18, 4:32 p.m., New York

"Angela!"

I awaken to see Lynne looking at me with a concerned expression. Everyone else in the room wears a variation of the same look.

"Angela, are you all right? You just passed out."

"Yeah, I'm fine. I'm really sorry." I begin to spew out my rehearsed answer to the questions that inevitably follow episodes such as this one. "I'm a narcoleptic. I'm sorry I didn't tell you before, but it's usually pretty under control."

"Well, do you want to go home, or are you feeling well enough to continue?"

"No, no, I'll be fine. Let's continue," I reply. And then my eyes close.

Tuesday, July 19, 1:33 a.m., Sacramento

Steve is shaking my shoulders.

"Honey, I'm sorry. I know you don't like to be disturbed at night, but Ella's really freaking out. She's sitting up in bed, and she's wailing about something, but she's still asleep. I need you."

"Steve, please," I beg. "For the love of God, please just wake her up, and tell her it's a dream, and stay next to her the rest of the night. I need to go back to sleep now."

"Angie, come on. I'm sick of this. I have a really important meeting at ten."

I'm almost crying. "Not now, please not now! We can talk about it tomorrow. I'm begging you."

Steve throws back the covers and stomps out of the room. I turn over and close my eyes.

Monday, July 18, 4:35 p.m., New York

Now everyone is clearly really worried. They are grouped around me, and someone is fanning me with a script.

I try to gather my thoughts. "I'm so sorry. This hasn't happened to me in a while. I'm okay now. I'll be fine. Um, so with Medea here, what I'm trying to do is to—"

Lynne cuts me off. "You know what? I would really like for you to go home and get some rest, okay? I just don't think you're in any condition to continue. Why don't we meet on Wednesday, just the two of us? Would two o'clock work for you?"

"Um...sure. I'll be there. I'm sorry, everyone."

I gather my things and scurry out of the room, my cheeks burning. I would think after all these years that I would be used to this, but it never really gets any easier.

Chapter 4

I WAS FIFTEEN years old, and the last place on earth I wanted to be was in the psychiatrist's office. He was on Eighty-First and Park, in an old brownstone a few blocks from Central Park. I would walk through the neighborhood, past children walking home from school with their nannies, and count the steps to the office door. It was six hundred steps from the subway. I remember how reluctantly I rang the bell—if my parents hadn't been checking in with the doctor, I never would have shown up to the appointments. In the office, I sat in the beige cracked leather chair and stared down Dr. Bailes.

"So, Angela, what would you like to talk about today?" he said.

"Nothing." I ran my tongue across my braces.

"Okay, well, how are you doing with your medication?"

"I don't need it. I'm not depressed."

Dr. Bailes smiled. His teeth were crooked.

"For gosh sakes," I said, "why can't you afford nicer furniture, with all the money my parents pay you?"

"I like my furniture. It's comfortable," he said. "Anyway, I didn't prescribe the Pamelor for depression, although it should help make you feel less anxious. I prescribed it because I think it may help with your narcolepsy. It's an off-label use. Do you know what that means?"

I rolled my eyes. "Yeah, duh, it means a different use than indicated on the label. I'm an honors student."

"Fair enough." Dr. Bailes took a deep inhalation of air and let it out slowly. "Have you noticed any difference?"

"No. Because I'm not a narcoleptic. I've told you—you've totally misdiagnosed me."

"Angela, it isn't just me. Your primary-care physician agrees. It's the only thing that makes sense. How else can your symptoms be explained?"

"Easy," I said as I peeled off a hanging bit of leather from the arm of my chair. "I live in parallel universes. I don't go to sleep. I just go to my other reality."

Dr. Bailes tugged on his gray mustache. "Sometimes narcoleptic people actually hallucinate. These 'visions' of your other life that occur when you fall asleep are most likely short hallucinations."

I sharply exhale. "Look, Dr. Bailes. I've read about narcolepsy. I don't have any muscle weakness, sleep paralysis, or exhaustion. I'm not narcoleptic. The only thing that happens is that I sometimes fall asleep during the day. And you want to know why? Because I *wake up* in my other life. Like right now, the me that lives in California is asleep in my bed. But if there was an earthquake, I might wake up, and that would make me fall asleep here in your office."

He wrinkled his forehead. "You have a strong fantasy life. Do you like to read science fiction?"

I knew he wouldn't understand. No one ever did. I could feel a lump rising in my throat, which meant I was going to cry, which meant that I was very angry.

"No! I do not like to read science fiction! I just want to be normal. Don't you get that? I don't want to go to bed and immediately wake up twelve hours later in my other life. I don't want two lives. And you know the worst part? The worst part is that you might be right, and if you're right, then one of my lives is just a dream. So who's not real? My baby cousin? My dog? Just tell me!"

"I'm going to tell you right now," he said firmly. "I am real. Your parents are real. You are real. Everything else, everything in your 'other life,' that's a dream."

"Okay," I said, standing up. "That's cool. There's just one problem. My psychiatrist in California, Dr. Tessler, she says that *you're* not real." A fat tear rolled down my cheek.

"Angie," said Dr. Bailes, "I admit that it is very unusual to have had the same continuous dream your entire life. And I can imagine that that could be very confusing. But I promise you that if you trust me, I can help you."

"Whatever," I said, picking up my backpack. "See you next week."

Chapter 5

Tuesday, July 19, 9:00 a.m., Sacramento

STEVE SLAMS HIS dresser drawer closed. "Yeah, I'm angry, Ang, and I'm tired. I have a really important meeting this morning with the Anderson Corporation. I need you to take a little of the burden with Ella at night. I can't keep doing this. I'm exhausted, and I'm burned out, and I'm the one who has to go be productive at work."

"Oh, because I do nothing productive at home, right?"

"You know that's not what I mean. But you can still cook dinner when you're tired. Or, hell, order a pizza…whatever you need to do. But I have to have my game on. Do you have any idea how many times this guy has changed his mind on me? I have to think on my toes here."

I frown. "I thought you were going with the open courtyard and the skylights and koi ponds and all that. 'Calm in the corporate world.'"

"Yeah, well, he hated that. So it's back to square one now."

"Sorry," I say. "I am. But you know it messes me up to be woken at night."

"I know, honey. The narcolepsy, I know. But I just…I'm at the end of my rope."

I try to think of some response that he will accept, but before I can reply, he's heading down the stairs.

"We'll talk tonight!"

After he leaves, I go about my day listlessly. I clean the downstairs bathroom, and after dropping Ella off at preschool, I pick up the many stuffed animals and dolls that litter her room. As I line them up on her bed, I plan dinner: steak and mashed potatoes. Steve will love that.

Later that afternoon, I step off the bus and walk the three blocks to Ella's preschool. After only a block, I can feel sweat trickling down my side. It is hot, the dry, searing heat of the Sacramento Valley. It's times like this that I really wish I could drive. As I approach Sutterville preschool, I see a line of cars entering the parking lot, parents here to pick up their toddlers.

I enter the building and scan the room for Ella. The preschool is essentially one large room divided into several different areas. There is a reading corner, a kitchen area, a puppet theater, and an art-activities station. Suddenly, something crashes into my butt, nearly knocking me forward onto the ground.

"Mommy!" Ella hugs me around my knees.

"Hi, baby," I say. "Whoa, let mommy go, okay?" I feel a hand on my shoulder and turn.

Ella's teacher, Miss Nishamura, is standing next to me, holding Ella's pink lunchbox with her embroidered monogram. She hands it to me.

"Oh, hi, Miss Nishamura. How was Ella today?"

"I have to tell you something about her, actually."

"Uh-oh," I say.

"No, no, it's really cute," she says, running her hand through her cropped black hair. "Today we went around and asked all the kids what their favorite food was. Everyone said basically the same thing: pizza, ice cream, or macaroni and cheese. Then we get to Ella, and she says, 'Shrimp risotto, asparagus, and a popsicle.'"

I laugh. "Yep, she's mama's little girl, all right."

"Tomorrow's your day to work here, right?"

"Yeah," I say. "I'm bringing the craft."

"Great, see you then," she says.

Ella's school is a cooperative preschool, so the parents act as assistant teachers; each parent comes in one day a week.

"Let's go, Mommy," says Ella, taking my hand.

When we get home, I start on dinner. Once everything is underway, I decide that we all need a little treat.

"Do you want to make chocolate-chip cookies for Daddy?" I call from the kitchen.

Ella comes running into the kitchen from the living room, her sock-clad feet padding on the linoleum.

"Yay!" Ella loves to help me cook. I love to cook too, which is why I'm getting Ella started young.

"Okay, honey, let's get you ready." I tie an old apron around her and grab a ponytail holder from the counter.

Ella snatches it from me. "I can do it." I let her try a few times, and then she hands it back to me.

I pull her hair out of her face and into a ponytail. Then I get a step stool for her to stand on.

I have her wash her hands while I get out the ingredients.

"Let's see now—first we need to sift the flour," I say.

She bounces up and down. "I can do it, Mommy. Please?"

I poke her tummy. "Sure, I'll measure it, and you can sift it."

We continue this way, with me measuring the ingredients and her mixing them. I also let her spoon the dough onto a cookie sheet. When I open the oven and go to put the cookies in though, she sticks out her lower lip.

"Let me, Mommy. My turn."

I shake my head. "Sorry, baby, but the oven is for grown-ups. Anyway, you did the hard part. Daddy will be so proud."

Ella grins. "I gotta color now!"

"Okay. Hey, I have an idea," I say. "Why don't you try using lots of colors this time, instead of just pink?"

"No. I like pink."

I smile. "Okay. Do you want me to color with you?"

"No. They're *my* pink crayons."

I tug softly on her brown pigtail. "All right, missy, go color."

She jumps off the step stool and runs upstairs.

As I cut into the steak to check if it is done, I hear the door unlock.

"Ella, Daddy's home," I call.

She responds immediately, tearing out of her room and down the stairs and propelling herself at Steve, hugging him around the legs.

"Daddy, Daddy, Daddy!"

Steve picks her up.

"How's Daddy's little girl today? Did you have fun at preschool?"

"I made the cookies! All by myself," she says.

"You made cookies at preschool?"

"No," I say, "I helped her make you some chocolate-chip cookies."

At dinner, Ella struggles with her steak.

Steve notices. "Hey, Elly, having a little trouble?" He leans over and cuts her steak into smaller pieces. Meanwhile, Ella forms a volcano with her mashed potatoes.

God, I love watching him with her. I love them both more than anything.

Suddenly, it starts to happen again. *Oh, no, not now. Please not now.* I breathe in and out, but I can't get enough air to fill my lungs. I gasp for air as the room lurches. My face tingles, and I feel my stomach turn, nausea washing over me in waves. I grip the table.

"Angie, what's wrong?" Steve puts his hand on mine.

"Panic attack," I say, gasping for air.

Steve's eyes relax. He must have thought I was choking. "It's okay, honey. Just breathe slowly. In and out…slowly. It will pass. Look in my eyes."

Poor Steve. He's become an experienced coach when it comes to my panic attacks. They started when Ella was born. They are the nagging thought, the fear, even the possible knowledge that my world doesn't really exist and that one day it may vanish like a puff of smoke.

I grip Steve's hand and force my breathing under control. I remind myself, as I have a hundred times before, that no one's life is secure. Anyone could die at any moment and lose everything. I'm no different. Still, I know I am different. I am definitely different.

I have to wait until Ella has had her bath and been put to bed before I finally get a chance to talk to Steve.

I walk into the living room, where Steve is watching TV.

I sit down beside him. "Honey, please, I want to talk to you."

"Look, Angie, I'm kind of tired. Why don't we talk tomorrow?"

"No, I want to deal with this now," I say.

Slowly, he turns off the TV and turns to face me on the couch.

"Why are you so mad at me?" I say. "I mean, I know you're stressed. But still. It's always been this way. You get up with Ella at night. You said you were okay with it."

He sighs. "Honey, I understand that it causes problems when your sleep is disturbed. But I'm going through a tough time now too. I need to be alert at work, and I just think you need to help a little with Ella at night."

I feel a lump forming in my throat. "Help a little with Ella? I'm sorry, but I am home with her every day. I am the one who has most of the burden. I'm the one who gave up my writing career. Not you."

"Hey," he says. "I never asked you to give up your career. You wanted to stay home. You cannot punish me for your decisions."

"No, I know it was my decision. But that's not the point. The point is that I do a lot for her. And I'm really sorry if it's a problem for you that I have a disease, but I do, and I'm not any happier about it than you are!"

Steve frowns. "It's interesting that you only have a 'disease' when it's convenient for you. The rest of the time you just live in parallel universes."

I shake my head. "No, you know what? You're right. I do believe that I live in parallel universes. I'm sick and tired of trying to explain away my symptoms as narcolepsy. So let's just go there. When Ella woke up last night, I was in the middle of my own important meeting, a meeting that was ruined by my falling asleep in the middle of it!"

Steve's eyes open wide. "So let me get this straight. You expect my actual career to suffer so that you don't fall asleep in your meeting in dreamland?"

That was mean. My eyes well up with tears. "Steve, don't belittle my life there. Don't you get it?" Tears now stream down my cheeks. "That world is just as real to me as this one. And if one of these worlds isn't real, it's just as likely to be this one. How do you think it feels to know that my husband and my child might be nothing more than a dream?"

Steve looks at me like I've slapped him in the face.

"I'm sorry, Steve, but how can I not fear that?" I wipe my nose on the back of my hand. "Are you going to say anything?"

"How am I supposed to respond when you tell me I'm not real?" he says. "Seriously, what am I supposed to think about having a wife who literally can't tell the difference between dreams and reality? That scares me. It scares me that you don't know that your daughter is real."

I grab his hand in mine. "What do you think it's like for me? You all feel equally real to me. You and Ella and…all of them too."

Steve looks deep into my eyes. "Okay, don't think right now. Just don't use your brain at all. Just look at me. Do you believe I'm real? Do you?"

I nod.

"Then I am real. And Ella is real, and our love is real. And you don't need to worry about anything else. Okay?"

"Okay," I say, letting him fold me into his arms.

"I love you."

I close my eyes. "I love you too."

Chapter 6

My Sacramento childhood was, in many ways, the polar opposite of my childhood in New York. My family lived in the suburbs. I rode my bike, I played on the levee near the Sacramento River, and I spent hours lying in the backyard, reading.

I remember leaving Mrs. Martinez's fifth-grade class and running to my mom's car in the parking lot, my book bag thumping against my thighs as my sneakers sank into the damp grass.

"Hey, Mom," I said, stepping into the front seat of our blue Honda Civic.

She brushed her long, light-brown hair from her face. I remember how she used to always wear peasant skirts. Like a hippie. It embarrassed me a lot.

"Hi, sweetie." She kissed me on the cheek, and I did a quick glance around to make sure none of my classmates saw the display of affection.

"Mom? Can we go get ice cream?"

"That depends. How much homework do you have?"

"Nothing, really. Not due tomorrow anyway. We have to do a report on our family history. It's due in a month though. I have to interview Grandma and Grandpa about their ancestors and stuff."

"That sounds neat." My mom pulled the car out and turned right. Yes! That meant we were headed toward Baskin-Robbins and not home. "We can call Grandma when we get home if you want, but we have to call before six, otherwise it will be nine o'clock there, and you know how early she goes to bed."

"Yeah." I picked at the pink polish on my pinky nail. "How come you and dad moved to California anyway?"

She smiled, and her eyes crinkled up. "We moved to San Francisco after college. We were hippies. And then Dad got his job teaching here, and we had you kids, and we just ended up staying. Trust me—you wouldn't like living in New York. It's so dirty and cold. You're lucky we moved." Huh. If only she knew.

We pulled into Baskin-Robbins. I already knew what flavor I would get. Blue Medal Ribbon with the chocolate ice cream and caramel swirls. Mmm…As we entered the store, I could smell the sweet waffle cones, and I knew that behind that glass counter were thirty-one flavors of bliss. Maybe I could get three flavors on a waffle cone. Just this once.

"Can I—"

"You can have a sugar cone," my mother said, "with one scoop."

My mom paid for the ice cream and stole a lick before handing me my cone.

"Hey, get your own!"

"Can't. I'm watching my figure."

As we walked out of the store, I saw the coolest car parked right out in front. It was some kind of sports car, red, and it looked more like a rocket than a car.

"Wow!" I said, running up and stroking the hood. "This is the kind of car I want to have when I turn sixteen."

"I don't think so," my mother said, taking my hand and pulling me toward our car.

"Why not?"

"Dad and I can't afford a car like that on a teacher and librarian salary."

"Then I'll get a job and buy it myself," I said. "I can work at Baskin-Robbins." I grinned, satisfied with my plan. It would be perfect. I would work every day after school, scooping cones (and eating as much ice cream as I wanted), and then I would drive home in my beautiful, shiny car. Everyone would beg me for a ride home. But I would only give rides to the cutest boys. And all of them would want to be my boyfriend.

"Buckle your seat belt." My mom took my cone so that I could buckle myself in. She stole another lick. "The problem is, Angie, that you aren't going to be able to drive."

"What?"

"Honey, it would be too dangerous. You could fall asleep at the wheel and crash." She paused. "You won't ever be able to drive."

I bit my lip. "It's not fair! I never get to do anything fun. I have to wear the dorky helmet when I ride my bike. I have to wear the life jacket when I swim. You don't even let me use the stove unless you're in the room! I'm not a baby."

My mother's eyes filled with tears. "I know. You're very mature. Don't you think I want to let you do all those things? But it isn't safe. I have to keep you safe."

Now I felt really guilty. I never even thought that it might be hard for my mom to have a daughter like me. "I know, Mom." I sighed. "It's okay. I understand."

But I didn't. I didn't understand why I was different.

Chapter 7

Friday, July 29, 9:00 p.m., New York

I'm at Slate, a bar and pool hall near my apartment, with Jana.

"What are you ladies drinking tonight?" our bartender says, leaning on the counter.

"I don't know yet," Jana says.

He smiles at her, taking in her curvy, barely five-foot frame, and his eyes linger on her chest.

"And you?" he says, barely glancing at me.

"Gin and tonic."

As he walks away, Jana whispers, "That is one good-looking man. He could be Taye Diggs's twin."

I agree with her and take out my wallet. Jana twirls a lock of blond hair around her finger. "I'm going to go home with him tonight."

I cough. "And there you go," I say. "I guess I'm on my own now."

"That's what I love about you, Angie. You know when to take a hint. And you attract different men than I do, with your different look."

"Is that supposed to be a compliment?" I say.

"No, yeah, of course. I mean, you're gorgeous, but you're so slim, and your hair is so dark—you just attract different guys than I do. That's all."

I shake my head. "Okay, well, have fun, and please be careful."

"Oh, I'll have fun," she says. "But I want you to have fun too. When's the last time you went on a date anyway? Four years ago?"

"I date!" I say. "Occasionally."

I leave twelve dollars on the bar and pick up my drink. I'm mildly annoyed. It isn't as if I begrudge Jana a good time. It's just that I would have liked to have had an actual conversation with her before being dismissed. Besides, my own relationship with men has been pretty complicated since I got married. I wasn't lying when I told Jana that I date—it's just that I don't have sex. I mean, I do. But only with Steve. On my wedding day, I made a vow that I would be true to Steve for the rest of my life. And breaking that vow, even here in my other life, just wouldn't feel right.

I make my way through throngs of people toward the pool tables. Feeling awkward and on display, I join the outskirts of a group of women watching a pool game in progress. I sip my drink. Then out of the corner of my eye, I see a tall man with olive skin and inexplicably bright-blue eyes staring right at me. His eyes are so blue that they can't possibly be real. *Colored contacts*, I think. I hold eye contact with him, and I feel my skin tingle all over. He looks as if he is appraising me, and I can't tell whether he is impressed or not. I smile weakly and then turn away, unable to hold his gaze any longer. I feel my cheeks burning. I want to leave, but I don't want him to watch me go. I feel frozen in place, and all I can do is look down into my drink at the little bubbles rising from the ice.

And then he is standing right next to me.

"Hi," he says. His voice is confident and deep. I look up and find myself staring deep into his eyes. He isn't wearing contacts.

"Hi," I say, in a near whisper.

He raises his lip into a half smile. "I think we just had a moment."

I laugh. I feel completely at ease.

"I'm Tony." He holds his hand out for me to shake.

"I'm Angela."

"Well, Angela, I apologize for staring, but you're very beautiful." He rubs his thumb along the side of my hand, and I feel electric sparks beneath his finger. The jolt of arousal is followed by an equally powerful jolt of guilt. *This isn't right.* But then again, what if I'm remaining faithful to a dream? *No.* I can't let myself think that way.

"I feel like I'm dreaming," Tony says. *So do I*, I think. Maybe *this* is a dream. And dreams don't count as cheating. I bite my lip and force myself down to earth.

"Thank you," I say. "But I should go."

He squeezes my hand. "Finish your drink first."

"Okay." I obey his order like a schoolgirl. What is the matter with me? I take a big gulp of my drink. The sooner I finish, the sooner I can make my escape.

"So, what do you do?" he says.

"I'm a costume designer for the theater."

"That's wonderful. I love the theater." He smiles, and I see that his teeth are white and straight. "I'm a writer."

"Oh, I used to be a journalist," I say, without thinking. *Other life, stupid.*

"Really? Where?"

I backtrack. "Well, just, um, in high school. For the school paper. I don't even know why I brought that up."

He laughs. "You're cute. Give me your phone number."

I take a deep breath. "I don't really think that's a good idea."

"Why not?" he says, "I'd love to take you out sometime, somewhere a little more private, where we can talk."

But that's just the problem. I don't trust myself to be alone with this man. Not at all.

"I'm sorry. I just don't date men that I meet in bars."

He hides a smile. "Okay, then we won't date. We'll just be friends."

Friends. That would be okay. Maybe. Against my better judgment, I hand him my card.

"See you soon," he says, brushing my chin with his thumb.

I feel the imprint of his touch long after he has left.

Tuesday, August 2, 5:37 p.m., New York

I am stir-frying some tofu and broccoli with soy sauce. The sizzling noise fills my apartment, and I know that anyone in the hallway can both smell and hear me cooking. As I turn the heat down slightly, the phone rings. I reach for my cell, on the counter next to me.

"Hello?"

"Hi, Angela. This is Tony, from the bar. How are you?"

My heart begins racing in my chest. I swallow hard. "I'm great, thanks. How are you?" I say. I had hoped he wouldn't call. Almost as much as I had hoped he would.

"I'm doing well. I just wanted to know if you'd like to have dinner with me this Friday."

"Sure, I'd love to." The words come out before I can consider what I am saying.

"Great. How about Sushi Samba at eight?"

"Okay, I'll meet you out in front."

"I can't wait to see you again," he says. And I have a feeling we are not going to be just friends.

Wednesday, August 3, 7:01 p.m., Sacramento

"Lullaby, my baby, lullaby for you. Lullaby, my baby, lullaby laloo." I am singing to Ella the same song my mother sang to me when I was little. The only problem is that it does not seem to be working tonight. Ella just will not close her eyes.

She giggles. "I'm not tired."

"Shh, no talking. Close your eyes," I say. I would love to leave her to fall asleep on her own, but Steve and I are really hoping for a little romance tonight. And that means that we need this little one asleep.

"Sing 'Kumbaya'!" Ella says.

I sigh. We're on our fifth lullaby, and we've already read nursery rhymes. But I need her asleep, or there is no hope of any privacy for me and Steve.

I sing. "Kumbaya, my Lord, Kumbaya."

Four verses in, Ella's eyes are closed and she has quieted. She has finally drifted off. I stand slowly and begin to turn toward the door.

"Sing 'Rock a Bye' again!" she says, her eyes popping open.

I take a deep breath just as Steve walks into the room, jingling his key chain.

"Okay, Ella-Bella. Get into the car. We're going for a drive."

Steve and I practically toss Ella into her car seat and then drive around the neighborhood for about half an hour, silently. Finally we hear heavy breathing coming from the backseat. As meticulously as if he were performing brain surgery, Steve parks the car and carries her into her bedroom, placing her gently into bed. She doesn't wake up. We look at each other, giddy with relief, and practically run to our bedroom.

There is no pretense as Steve tears off my clothes. It's been too long.

We skip right to the main event, and in under an hour, we've had sex, brushed our teeth, gotten into our pajamas, and settled into bed. We may not have a lot of time together, but we still love each other just as much as we did in Steve's Spartan dorm room.

Chapter 8

AT FIFTEEN YEARS old, I was *in love* with Dan Mitchell. He had bleached-blond hair and green eyes, and at six feet, he was a full six inches taller than I was. He was also a senior. He dressed in black, most of the time, and wore combat boots to school. He was utterly cool and utterly off limits.

"No dating until you're sixteen," my dad said. And he was serious.

"It's not fair!" I said. "In California, you guys don't even care when I date. But no one there has asked me out! You just want to ruin my life!"

"Yes," my dad said, sighing. "It's true, Angela. Every day I wake up and try to think of what I can do to completely ruin your life."

"Dad, I love him! I would do anything for him!" I was sobbing with the angst that only a fifteen-year-old could maintain on a daily basis.

My dad's eyes widened. "And that is *exactly* why you are not allowed to date him."

After days of wheedling, however, I did convince my parents that I should be allowed to go on a group date. Not even a date, a group outing, I promised them. We would go see a movie and have pizza and then come home. Even my dad had to admit that was pretty tame.

Of course, he had no idea that I let Dan get to second base during the movie.

Over the next couple of weeks, I lost myself in the excitement of being with Dan. Even on our group dates, we found ways to be alone together. On a walk in Central Park, we broke off from the group and groped behind a tree. On the subway on the way home from school, I sat on his lap and we made out, to the silent stares of unfazed New Yorkers.

"Angie," Dan said one spring day, squeezing my left breast behind the school, "What do you think about teenagers having sex?"

I blushed. I couldn't believe he was asking me this. Did he want me to have sex with him? What was I supposed to say? I swallowed. "I don't know. I mean, I guess if they really love each other, then it's probably okay. I mean, you know, like if they are going to get married after high school."

Dan smiled. "Are you in love with me?"

I picked a daisy that was growing next to the crumbling brick wall of the school. I knew this was a trick question. I had learned from *Seventeen* magazine that you were never supposed to admit to a guy that you loved him before he said he loved you. It gave him too much power. And even if he said it, you were supposed to say "Thanks for telling me that. I care about you deeply" and then wait a little longer before you said it back. But the magazine never said what you were supposed to say if he actually asked you. I stalled for time.

"Are you in love with me?" I said.

"I asked you first," he said, grinning.

"I care about you deeply," I said.

He nodded. "Yeah, that's what I thought. I love you too."

Whoa. My head was swirling. Aside from the fact that he had clearly misinterpreted what "care deeply" meant, this was the most wonderful moment of my life so far. He loved me! Dan Mitchell, who had two tattoos and three piercings and was seventeen years old, was *in love* with me.

He kissed me, and his lips were soft. "I want to be inside you," he whispered.

My heart started racing. "I don't know, Dan," I said. "I'm only fifteen. I don't really feel ready for that yet."

"But, Angie, we need to find out if we're sexually compatible if we're going to get married after high school."

Married? I wasn't sure if I had heard him right.

"You want to marry me? For real?"

"Yeah," he said, "I do."

"Are you going to get me a ring?"

"Um, here," he said, pulling a silver ring from his pinky and putting it on my ring finger. "Now…it's official."

I bit my lip. I felt giddy, like I imagined it would feel to be drunk. And then the school bell rang, and lunch was over. I stood up and picked up my backpack.

"Wait, Ang. I have an idea," he said. "Let's ditch fifth period and go to my house. My parents aren't home, so we'll have the place to ourselves all afternoon. I want your first time to be special." He kissed me again and took my hand.

My stomach lurched. I really didn't know if I was ready for this. But I wanted to marry Dan more than anything. And if we were going to get married, we had to know whether we were sexually compatible. Didn't we?

Chapter 9

Friday, August 5, 9:00 p.m., New York

I TAKE A bite of tres leches cake and wash it down with a sip of champagne. I look up to find Tony staring into my eyes. I wonder what it would be like to kiss him.

The date has been perfect. Tony has said all the right things. He writes for the *New Yorker* and has had a book of poetry published. I'm impressed by his knowledge of theater and the New York art scene. He says he is close to his parents. Best of all, he seems to find me equally interesting.

The server hands Tony the check, and when I offer to pay half, he refuses. He does allow me to pay the tip after a small amount of arguing. I leave a generous amount, remembering my days as a waitress in college.

When we step outside, it's still warm out. I am wearing white linen pants and a blue top, and I don't even need the little sweater I brought. As we walk, Tony puts his hand on the small of my back. Again, I feel a jolt of electric energy running through my body.

We end up in the bar at the W Hotel, having a few drinks. Actually, I only have one because I'm already slightly buzzed from the champagne. In a booth in a corner, Tony puts his arm around me.

"I'm really glad I asked you out," he whispers.

"Me too." I look at his lips. He licks them as he leans in toward me.

Reluctantly, I pull away. I want nothing more than to kiss in the bar like drunken college students. Still, it just doesn't feel all right. But it doesn't feel all wrong either.

"It's getting late," I say. Luckily, though, I am able to stay up pretty late in my New York life. As long as I'm asleep by eleven or so, thanks to the difference in time, I can be up bright and early at eight for my life in Sacramento with Ella.

"I'll walk you home."

As we walk toward my apartment, my mind races. Steve doesn't even believe that this world is real, and I have to admit that he certainly wouldn't care if I "cheat" on him here. Besides, it seems ridiculous that I should have to be single for the rest of my life here just because I'm married over there. I realize with a jolt that I actually feel happy right now. And the truth is that I haven't felt this excited about a man here in New York since I was with Dan in high school.

"What are you thinking about?" Tony says.

"Nothing. Just that I like you." *I really like you.*

He laughs. "You're adorable."

On the stoop of my building, he kisses me. He nuzzles against my ear, and I feel his hot breath on my neck. "Can I come up?"

I intend to say no. But then he kisses me again, and I feel my reason melting away. *We'll just kiss*, I tell myself.

"Okay, but just for a few minutes," I say out loud.

We kiss all the way up in the elevator. Once in my apartment, clothes rapidly start flying off. *We'll just kiss naked*, I tell myself. I feel a strong tinge of guilt. Poor Steve. But Steve doesn't ever have to know. I have a different life here.

Soon, Tony and I are tangled up in the sheets. And it's good. Very good. Every sensation is new and amazing to me. The smell of his skin alone sends shivers up my spine, and I wonder how it is that I've gone four years (at least here) without having sex.

Saturday, August 6, 1:00 p.m., Sacramento

I'm laughing so hard I can barely catch my breath. Ella and my parents' dog, both of whom are roughly the same size, are rolling in the grass together, Martin licking all over Ella's face. It's hot, but in the shade on my parents' deck, it feels just bearable enough that we all decided to sit out in the backyard. I'm so glad that we live near enough to my parents to come over frequently. I love the fact that Ella gets to play in the playhouse my dad built for me when I was a kid, and to pick the honeysuckle growing over the fence, and to chew on the mint leaves in mom's garden.

Ella runs to me, her eyes dancing. "Mommy, when does my puppy come? When?"

I glance at Steve. We've discussed the puppy situation for weeks now. I happen to agree with Ella on the topic. If it were up to the two of us, we'd probably be raising two puppies, a kitten, and maybe a hamster or two. Steve, however, would prefer that we wait on the puppy until Ella is a little older.

"Ell, next Christmas you can ask Santa to bring you a puppy, okay?" he says.

"When is Christmas?" She tilts her head.

"In about four months," I say.

"How many cartoons is that?" She narrows her eyes. My dad laughs.

"Well, that's a lot of cartoons, young lady," he says, taking a swig of his beer. "But you can play with Martin all you want until you get your own puppy."

Ella goes to Dad and climbs on his lap. "Grandpa, what kind of beer is that?"

"Corona."

"Grandpa Tom, I want Corona!" she says, clapping her hands.

"Sorry, kid," he says. "In about eighteen years I'll be happy to give you one."

Ella's eyes begin to fill with tears. Now we're in for it. Before I have a second to react, Ella is facedown on the deck, screaming and kicking her legs. "I want beer. I want beer!"

My dad shrugs. "Sorry, guys."

"It's not your fault. She's just at that age. Unfortunately, I haven't figured out how to get her to stop once she gets like this."

My mom stands up and puts her hands on her hips. "Uh-oh," she says loudly, "I forgot about the brownies in the house. I was going to give them to a certain little girl, but I guess she'd rather cry on the deck than have brownies."

Like lightning, Ella's head pops up, her lip quivering. "Brownies?"

"Yeah," my mom says. "But I need your help to put them on the plate. We can't have brownies unless you come inside and help me."

Ella considers this briefly and then runs after my mom.

A few minutes later, they return with a plate of homemade brownies.

Once Ella is absorbed in her brownie, my mom takes me aside. "Well, I guess things with Ella aren't any better, then?"

I sigh. "No, Mom, honestly, she's usually pretty good. She cries when Steve goes to work, but otherwise she usually listens pretty well."

"Really? Because a moment ago she was writhing on the floor like she was having an epileptic fit."

"It's just that she hasn't been sleeping well. She's been having these night terrors every couple of nights, and she's tired and cranky."

My mom pats my arm. "Honey, why don't you let her sleep with you?"

I look pointedly at her. "Mother, you know I can't have Ella waking me up in the middle of the night."

"Well, yes," she says, "but you've been doing pretty good lately, haven't you? Not too many episodes?"

I almost tell her about what happened at my production meeting the other day. But it's fruitless. I shrug. "Well, I won't do well at all if she sleeps with me. Trust me."

That night in bed, Steve and I cuddle after leaving Ella asleep in her room, her eyelids covered in a sheen of dewy baby sweat. It feels so good to be here with Steve. As I close my eyes, I think of Tony. I feel so guilty, but at the same time, Tony seems so far away right now. Almost like a dream, I suppose. If I had any idea what a dream was like.

The here and now is solid. Steve is solid. And he's mine. He falls asleep so quickly. I look up at his face, and I love him so much I almost want to cry. God, I'm lucky.

Chapter 10

I NEVER LIKED to take notes. I knew that writing down the precious words of the professor was considered mandatory by most students, but I found it hard to fully listen to what was currently being said when I was occupied with writing down what had *already* been said. Nevertheless, I needed something to do with my hands. I tried knitting, but I quickly gave that up after a few pointed stares from my sociology instructor. Now I had nothing to do but pick dirt out from under my fingernails.

"...and that is what I mean when I refer to a social construct," Professor Knight said.

I now moved on to my cuticles, biting at a hangnail.

"So please be sure that you have finished reading chapter four as well as the assigned reading in your course pack before the next class. We're going to have a discussion, and I may be calling on anyone."

I stood up, smoothing my black skirt. Then I grabbed my bag and headed toward the door, getting caught in the cluster of other students.

"I was wondering," a voice said, "if you might want to borrow my notes. Since you obviously didn't take any."

I looked up, startled, into the warm and smiling eyes of a tall, broad-shouldered guy.

"Oh, um, that's okay," I said.

"I'm sorry. I don't mean to be rude. It's just that you never even looked at the teacher once. It was funny. And I get it, because I do the same thing. I space out. But not today. Today I took really copious notes. So anyway, I thought maybe you might want to borrow them, and then on Thursday it can be your turn to take notes while I daydream."

I laughed. "That's not a bad idea, actually."

He ripped the pages from his notebook and handed them to me. "Here ya go. I'm Steve, by the way."

"Angela," I said, holding out my hand to shake his. He was cute. A little overly friendly maybe, but cute. And for some reason, he wasn't shaking my hand.

"Um, your, uh, your finger's bleeding," he said.

"Oh, I'm sorry." I hastily pulled my hand away and tried to hide it from sight. How disgusting.

But instead of walking away, he reached into his bag and pulled out a Band-Aid.

"Here, give me your hand."

I held out my hand, and when he touched me, I stopped breathing. Steve carefully bandaged my finger. "All better," he said.

I inhaled sharply. "Do you always carry Band-Aids?" I said.

He shook his head, laughing. "Yeah. I'm pretty uncoordinated. I'm always injuring myself."

I laughed. He was funny. And the way he looked at me made me feel beautiful.

"Actually," he said, "wanna get some food? I was going to get my hair cut, but I'd much rather grab a burger and get to know you better."

"I don't know," I said, wrinkling my nose in mock disgust. "Your hair is looking a little scraggly. Maybe you should keep that haircutting date and call me tomorrow."

He frowned. "You're right. I'm not going to take you out looking like this. You are not the kind of girl you take out for burgers. You are the kind of girl you take out for steak."

I giggled and shook my head. "No, really, I was just kidding. Please, you don't have to get your hair cut just for me. And burgers are fine."

"No, no, I want to," he said. "And I really do want to take you out for steak." He looked down at his shoes. "I've been trying to get up the nerve to talk to you since the first day of class, actually."

Without thinking, I put my hand on his shoulder. "Well, I would love to go out with you."

Chapter 11

Saturday, August 6, 2:00 p.m., New York

I'M SITTING ON the couch writing in my journal, and I'm reeling with the intensity of my date with Tony. Yet I still can't help feeling that he is almost too perfect to be true. So of course, I Google him. Twenty results appear on the screen. The first five are reviews of his poetry book, titled simply *Poems*. A moment later, I've ordered the book from Amazon. It will be delivered within the hour. One of the definite advantages of living in New York City is that I can have anything from a DVD to a cupcake to a book delivered to my home in under an hour. As I continue sifting through the websites, I see that his book got very respectable reviews. The *New York Times* says, "A quirky and illuminating look at life in a postmodern world." The *New Yorker* writes, "A guilty pleasure you don't have to feel guilty about." God, I'm dating a poet. I feel my stomach lurch like a kid swinging high in the air. I need to stop.

But of course, I don't. The next several results are links to articles he's written for the *New Yorker*. I read an article he has written about his childhood in Greece and the influence of poetry on his life. I wonder if someday I'll go to his home in Greece with him, meet his family...

Two hours later, I'm curled up on the couch with a copy of his book. *An impermeable shell surrounds me, for I'm a stoic, hard and strong*...I pause. My eyes hurt. Maybe it's time to stop analyzing this man I've just met. I'm feeling very sleepy; I close my eyes. Maybe it's as simple as: I like him, and he likes me.

Sunday, August 7, 3:01 a.m., Sacramento

I haven't been able to sleep for two hours. I'm really hot and thirsty. For me, a nap in one life means insomnia in the other. Not fun. Steve, of course, is sleeping peacefully beside me. I'm sweaty, and I feel like I'm swallowing cotton. I turn over, but it's no use.

"Where you going, honey?" Steve mumbles.

"Bathroom."

I stumble out of bed and into the master bathroom. I look at myself in the mirror. My hair is all messy. I smooth it with my hand and fill a little Dixie cup with water. After five cupsful, I decide I should probably use the bathroom before heading back to bed. On the toilet, the world begins to spin.

Saturday, August 6, 6:05 p.m., New York

The telephone ringing jars me awake.

"Hello?"

"Hi, beautiful. I didn't wake you up, did I?" It's Tony. His voice alone makes my heart flutter.

I smile and bite my lip. "No, no, I was just…reading."

"I wanted to thank you for the wonderful time last night."

"Yeah," I say, grinning so wide that I'm glad he can't see me. "I had a really amazing time too."

"Good, because I can't get you out of my head. What are you reading?"

I glance down at his book, still in my hand. "Oh, just *Medea*. Trying to get a little work done."

"Well, how would you like to go get some brunch tomorrow? I want to see you again."

"Yeah, brunch sounds great."

"Okay, I'll come by and pick you up at noon."

"Sounds wonderful. I'll see you tomorrow," I say.

Sunday, August 7, 3:10 a.m., Sacramento

Steve finds me asleep on the toilet. I hate my life.

Saturday, September 24, 3:34 p.m., Sacramento

"Ella, if you stick your finger in that cake, I swear you will go to your room."

Ella looks up at me with wide eyes, her finger paused in midair, about to strike at the whipped cream on Steve's flourless chocolate birthday cake.

"I'm just loving it," she says, wrinkling her forehead.

"Loving it?"

"Yeah, I'm…um…I'm petting him."

I laugh, shaking my head. "Okay, honey, cakes aren't dogs. They don't need to be petted. Why don't you go get Daddy's present from under my bed and bring it down here?"

Ella runs upstairs just as the phone rings.

"Hi, Mom, have you guys left yet?"

"Well, I'm on my way. Your dad isn't feeling very well, so he's staying home. He didn't want to get anyone else sick."

"Oh, that's too bad."

"Yeah, well, you know your father," she says. "He doesn't take good care of himself. Are Bill and Linda there yet?"

"Not yet. They called a few minutes ago," I say. "They'll be here in about a quarter of an hour."

Fifteen minutes later, on the dot, the doorbell rings. Steve's parents, Bill and Linda, are standing outside holding gifts. I give them each a hug and open the door wider.

"Hi, Angie, how are you?" Linda says. Ella peeks out from behind my legs. "And how's my little Ellie bear?"

"Say hi to Grandma and Grandpa," I say, picking Ella up.

"Hi!" She grins widely. Bill and Linda kiss her.

"Hey," Bill says, "don't wipe off my kiss."

"I'm just rubbing it in," she says. We all laugh as Steve enters the room, holding a tray of shrimp appetizers.

As we settle in on the couch, Steve's sister, Janelle, arrives with her latest boyfriend. He looks so similar to her last boyfriend that for a moment I think she's joking when she introduces him as Zeke.

"Hi, Zeke," Steve says, holding out his hand. "Nice to meet you."

I catch Steve's eye, and we smile at each other. This guy will be lucky if Janelle lets him hang around until after cake.

Soon, my mom arrives. "Hi everyone," she says as she lets herself into the house. "Oh, hi, Janelle. I didn't know you and Mark were coming."

I shudder. "Mom, this is Zeke, Janelle's *new* boyfriend."

"What? You're not Mark? But you look just like him!"

I shoot my mom a look, and she shrugs. "Sorry. I'm sure you're a much better catch than he was." She pats Zeke on the shoulder and heads into the kitchen, depositing her gift on the counter. "Happy Birthday, Steve," she says, hugging him.

After dinner, we sit around the living room and watch Steve open his presents. He looks so happy right now, surrounded by everyone who loves him. I wish I could be with everyone who loves me all at the same time, but unfortunately, that will never happen.

Chapter 12

Tuesday, October 11, 12:30 p.m., Sacramento

Ella and I are walking through Jo-Ann Fabric, trying to find something for her Halloween costume. This is the first year she is really aware of what's going on, and she really has her heart set on an amazing costume. Luckily for Ella, although she doesn't know it, I am a costume designer in New York. And not only can I design, but I can sew as well. We walk among the racks of multicolored fabrics, weaving through velvets and chiffons. I reach out and touch a soft purple iridescent fabric that reminds me of fairy wings. Fairy wings…

"Mommy?"

"Yes, sweetie?"

"I wanna be the sparkliest princess ever in the whole world, okay?"

"Don't worry, baby," I say. "You'll be very sparkly."

"And pink. Pink and sparkly."

I glance back at the purple fabric. "Are you sure you don't want wings?"

She looks at me like I'm stupid. "Mommy, I'm being a princess. Not a fairy. Plus, I said pink!"

"Right, okay, how about this?" I pull out a bolt of pink glittery tulle with little rhinestones glued all over it.

Ella gazes at the fabric as though it is the Holy Grail. "My dream came true," she says, whispering.

As the Jo-Ann employee cuts the pink tulle for me, I glance back at the purple fabric. It would be absolutely perfect for *A Midsummer Night's Dream*, which I'm designing for the Shakespeare Theater in Washington, DC. I've been searching every fabric store in the New York area for a swatch of material to use for wings for Titania, the fairy queen, and I haven't been able to find anything. How on earth, I wonder, could the perfect fabric be out here in Sacramento? Not what I would have expected. Still, it's not a problem. I'll just call this Jo-Ann store tomorrow from New York and have the fabric shipped to me. Funny how I can help myself in my other life. It's times like these that I almost appreciate my peculiar situation.

Tuesday, October 11, 4:25 p.m., New York

"No, it's purple. Iridescent. Um, it sort of looks like what fairy wings could be made out of?"

I'm on the phone with an employee of Jo-Ann, and the conversation is not going well.

"No, I'm sure that you have it," I say, trying to hide the frustration in my voice. "I was in your store today, and I saw it."

"Ma'am, I'm sorry, but all I see is this purple chiffon here, and if that's not what you mean, then I'm afraid I can't help you. Why don't you come back in and look for it?"

"Because I'm…" I stop myself before I say "in New York." "Because I'm too busy. I'll, um, I'll come in tomorrow. Bye."

Wednesday, October 12, 3:43 p.m., Sacramento

I storm into Jo-Ann Fabric, carrying Ella. I can see the purple fabric from across the room. I have an urge to buy it, even though it won't do me any good.

"See, I told you you had it," I say to the saleslady. "I don't know what the problem was."

She stares at me blankly, and I want to kick myself. Of course this woman has no idea what I'm talking about.

"Just talking to myself," I say before I turn and leave the store.

I have to be sure to memorize the fabric reference number so that I can buy this stuff when I'm back in New York.

As Ella and I climb into the bus, she scowls at me.

"What's wrong with you, sourpuss?" I tap her on the nose.

"I said no wings," she says.

I laugh. "I know, El. This fabric is for Mommy. You won't have wings. I promise."

Wednesday, October 12, 3:02 p.m., New York

I'm sitting on the floor, feeling extremely dejected. Not only have I called Jo-Ann (this time with the reference number), but I've also called every fabric store in New York and looked online. I can't find any store that carries this fabric. Finally, in desperation, I call the manufacturer.

"Hi," I say to the woman who answers the phone. "Listen, I'm having the hardest time finding a store that carries your number R39778022366Q fabric. Can you check on that for me, or could I possibly order some directly from you?"

I am met with silence.

"Sorry, what was that number?" she says in a monotone voice.

I repeat the number.

"I'm sorry, ma'am, but we have no such fabric. That reference number is not in our database."

I hang up, stifling the urge to throw the phone across the room. The fabric doesn't exist. I have to leave tomorrow for Washington, DC, to show the director my sketches and fabric swatches, and I still have nothing for the wings.

Thursday, October 13, 7:09 p.m., Sacramento

With manic energy, I sew the purple and apparently nonexistent fabric into the most beautiful pair of nonexistent wings you ever saw.

Ella walks into my bedroom, takes one look at the wings, and runs downstairs to Steve, crying all the way.

A few minutes later, I hear Steve's footsteps on the stairs.

"Honey," he says, "I think you're being a little controlling about Ella's Halloween costume. She's pretty upset. She said you're forcing her to wear purple wings."

I start to laugh and then to cry, both at the same time, clutching the wings to my chest. What is wrong with me? I shouldn't be reacting like this, but I feel as if months of frustration have been building up inside me. I'm tired of people thinking that I'm crazy. And worse, I'm afraid that I really am crazy.

Steve stares at me. "Ang, I really think you need to get a grip about this. I told her she doesn't have to wear them. It's not fair to force her if she doesn't want to."

"No," I say, gasping for air. "Poor little Ella. They're for me."

"Oh." Steve smiles at me and touches my chin. "You're going to be a fairy for Halloween?"

"No," I say, standing up and leaning against him. "It's just that I have this really important design meeting tomorrow in New York, and I wanted to use this fabric for the wings I'm designing, but it turns out that apparently this fabric doesn't exist there. And now, apparently, I'm having a bit of a mental break." I laugh and then cough. "Do you have any idea how frustrating that is for me?"

Steve looks at me sadly. "I don't think I could possibly understand how frustrating things are for you, baby."

Monday, October 31, 5:30 p.m., Sacramento

Ella and Steve are getting ready to go trick or treating around the block. I'm staying here and passing out candy. I've decided to wear my purple fairy wings with a black dress. Ella looks positively angelic in the little dress I made her. It has a tight pink satin bodice and, of course, the giant pink sparkly skirt. I even made her a little bejeweled tiara.

My mom and dad are here to take pictures before Steve and Ella go.

"Turn to me, princess," says my dad, looking to Ella.

She giggles and poses for the camera.

"You're a little ham, aren't you?" my mom says, shaking her head.

"I'm not a ham. I'm a princess!" Ella says.

I laugh and give her a big kiss on her fat little cheek. Soon, Ella and Steve are out in the night along with the throngs of other kids and parents outside.

"Are you guys going to hang around for a little while?" I say, turning to my parents.

My mom looks at my dad. "No, hon, I didn't even think we should have come to begin with. Your dad is still really feeling under the weather."

"Still? It's been almost a month. Are you okay, Dad?"

"Oh, I'm fine," he says, frowning. "You know how your mom worries. The doctor thinks I might have mono. I have to go in for some tests tomorrow."

"Mono? Have you been kissing other women, Dad?" I playfully push his shoulder.

"Just your mom," he says, and I notice for the first time how truly old he looks.

Chapter 13

I LOST MY virginity to Dan. It wasn't really the way I thought it would be. I had always imagined being a bride, my husband carrying me over the threshold of our honeymoon suite. There would be candles all around the room and rose petals sprinkled on the bed. My husband would remove my white dress, there would be a brief moment of pain, and then...I would be a woman.

The reality was nothing like I had imagined. Dan and I arrived at his parents' apartment and went into his bedroom.

"Do you want some music on?" he said.

"Um, okay." I was already having doubts. My mind raced through everything that could go wrong. What if it hurt really badly? What if I got pregnant? My heart started to beat so quickly I thought I might pass out.

Dan turned on his CD player, and heavy-metal music filled the room.

I felt my skin go hot and my eyelids prickle. Oh God, I was definitely going to be sick. I ran to the bathroom, just in time, and emptied the contents of my lunch into the toilet. What was the matter with me? I was acting like such a child! *Don't humiliate yourself,* I thought. *You are going to do this.* I pictured myself walking down the aisle with Dan at my side. I pictured the beautiful children I would have with Dan. *Yes, this is the right thing to do.* I breathed in and out deeply, and then I rinsed my mouth with wintergreen Scope and returned to the bedroom.

Dan's floor was so covered in clothing and food wrappers that I could hardly see the carpet. On his wall were various posters of Kiss, by the far wall was his dresser, and next to it was his bed. There, on the single bed, was Dan... completely naked.

I gasped.

"Hey, babe, you all right?" he said.

I nodded, swallowing hard. Dan walked toward me and removed my white tank top. *At least I'm wearing white,* I thought. He pulled me toward the bed, kissed me, fondled my breasts, and then put on a condom.

"Ready?" he said.

No! No, I was not ready. Not ready at all. But what was I supposed to do? If I said no, he would never marry me. I would never have the wonderful life I imagined. I forced my lips into a smile.

"Yes," I said.

I remained absolutely silent through the pain, but I felt like I was screaming inside. *Please, God, let this be over soon.* Luckily for me, being an overly excited teen-aged boy, Dan was finished in under a minute. But when he stood up, I could tell by the look on his face that something was wrong.

"What is it?" I said. I wondered if I had been bad at it. Maybe I was supposed to do something other than just lie there.

"You're bleeding," he said.

"Well, I'm a virgin. I mean, I was a virgin. That's what happens. Didn't you pay attention in health? I thought you'd had sex before."

His eyes were wide. "Yeah, but not with a virgin." He turned away. "It's just...a lot of blood."

I sat up and looked at the bed. My chest tightened. His sheets were soaked in blood...soaked. "Oh my gosh," I said, and I started to cry.

The whole way home, Dan was silent. He couldn't even look at me.

Chapter 14

Tuesday, November 1, 7:00 p.m., New York

THE NIGHT IS cool and crisp in New York. Tony and I walk toward Union Square, my heels clicking on the pavement as we navigate through all the other people on the street. The Empire State Building is white tonight, my favorite; it looks the most elegant that way. I hold Tony's arm as we walk into Blue Water Grill.

As the hostess seats us in a cozy booth upstairs, Tony squeezes my hand.

"Did I tell you how absolutely ravishing you look tonight?" he says.

I smile, glad he noticed the difference. I'm wearing a strapless, deep-pink dress with black stilettos, and I've even straightened my hair. My normal casual look and my naturally wavy hair are gone, replaced by a sleek and sexy me.

"No, I don't recall that you did," I say.

"Well, you do. Happy birthday."

"Thanks." I note that in the candlelight, Tony looks even more handsome than usual. I feel suddenly shy. He stares at me so intently sometimes that it can be unnerving.

When the server comes, Tony orders a bottle of pinot grigio and a goat-cheese and pear salad for us to share.

Since we first started dating, Tony and I have seen each other at least once a week. He takes me out for nice dinners that I could never afford on my artist's salary, and he never lets me pay for anything. Even better, he has a gorgeous apartment down in Battery Park City overlooking the river.

The first time I went home with him, he unlocked the door with his little electronic key, and when we stepped inside, my breath was nearly taken away.

Before me was an entire wall made of windows, overlooking Battery Park and the river. And…the apartment was huge. I audibly gasped and turned to him.

"You like it?" he said.

"Um, yeah! What's not to like? You have a brand-new apartment with a gym and a dishwasher and a view. And"—I looked down the long hallway—"just how many bedrooms do you have?"

"Four," he said, blushing. "And two bathrooms."

"Two bathrooms?" I was in awe. I had never dated someone with two bathrooms before. "I am now so truly embarrassed that you have seen the shoe box that I live in."

He cupped my face in his hands. "Don't be embarrassed. You are an artist."

"Well, you're a writer. The difference is that you are highly successful at what you do."

He frowns. "And so are you. But you're just getting started. You should be proud. And someday, who knows…Trust me. I had an apartment half that size not so long ago."

At the Blue Water Grill, I order the miso-glazed sea bass, my favorite. Tony brushes my hair behind my ear.

"I was thinking, Angela, maybe we could spend a little more time together before you have to go to DC for tech week."

"Sure, more time together would be great," I say, smiling.

"Well, good, because I was thinking maybe we could go away for the weekend. Vermont is beautiful this time of year."

Suddenly, I am gripped by panic. I've purposely kept our dates to very specific blocks of time when I know I'm deep asleep in California. I breathe in, my insides feeling shaky. I've wanted to put off this conversation for as long as possible. It's hard for men to understand the severity of my condition unless they experience its ill effects firsthand. And now it looks like I'm about to have to revisit my least favorite topic of discussion.

"Listen, Tony," I say. "I don't know if that would be the best idea. I just have a lot of work to do. I'm also designing *Mysterious Religion* at the Public, and I have a lot of research to do."

"Oh, okay," he says, looking down at his plate.

The sea bass feels mealy in my mouth. I put my fork down.

"Tony, this is truly not a rejection of you. It…it isn't you. It's me."

"Whoa. Are you breaking up with me?" he says, his eyes widening.

"No, God no. This is hard. Listen. I'm just going to be honest with you, okay? I am a narcoleptic. The reason I haven't spent all that much time with you is that I didn't want you to find out."

"Oh." He looks relieved. "Okay, so what does that mean for you?"

You have no idea. "Well, it means that I randomly fall asleep at very inappropriate times. It means that I could fall asleep while walking down the street, while riding a bike, while having sex."

He raises his eyebrows.

"I'm serious, buddy. It's happened before, and it will happen again. But the only way I have the disease under control is if I get twelve hours of sleep every night, generally from around ten or eleven p.m. until ten or eleven the next morning. But sometimes, it happens anyway."

"Sounds like a pretty nice cure, if you ask me," he says, squeezing my hand.

"It's not a cure, just a prevention," I say. "It's is also a very dangerous disease. I can't drive. I rarely ride a bike. I'm afraid every time I cross a busy street. It's not easy for me."

"I'm sorry," Tony says, his eyes full of sympathy. "I didn't mean to joke about it. You must have a very difficult life."

"I do," I say. "But I make it work. The question is, can you handle it? Can you handle never waking me up during that time? Can you protect me if I fall asleep in a dangerous situation? If it's too much for you, I understand. I do."

"No." He takes my hand. "It's not too much for me. We can deal with this together."

I smile and squeeze his hand. "Thank you."

Just then, the server arrives with two glasses of champagne and a piece of cake.

"I told them it was your birthday when I made the reservation," Tony says. "Don't worry. They promised no one would sing."

As we sip champagne in the flickering candlelight, Tony takes a small box out of his coat pocket and hands it to me. I open it and gasp. Inside is a pair of sterling-silver earrings with giant square citrine stones, my birthstone. They must have cost him a lot of money.

"Oh, Tony, these are absolutely beautiful. Thank you so much."

"Put them on," he says, beaming.

And I do, even though they clash terribly with my pink dress.

Tony takes a sip of his champagne and licks his lips. "Angela, I think I might be falling in love with you."

"I'm falling in love with you too, Tony," I say.

That night, I call Jana on the phone.

I tell her everything that happened, including Tony's gift to me.

"Wait—I thought you hated your birthstone," Jana says.

"Well, it isn't that I hate it. I just don't really like orange all that much. But I don't know. I think every woman should own something in her birthstone. Besides, it was really the perfect gift. My birthstone on my birthday. And he spent a lot of money. I know he did."

"Well, it's the thought that counts anyway," she says.

"Exactly. And he said he loves me. That's the important part."

"Well..."

"What?"

"Nothing."

"No, Jana, you're holding something back. What is it?"

She sighs. "Look—I don't mean to burst your bubble, but he didn't exactly say he loves you. He said he thinks he might be falling in love with you. There is a difference."

"Okay, Jana, could you please be happy for me?" I say. "So what if he is just falling and hasn't fallen yet? I'm not sure I'm fully in love with him yet either. It's a process. And he is letting me know where he is, which I think is pretty amazing, given that I'd just told him all about my narcolepsy."

"I know. I know. I'm sorry. I wasn't trying to say he's an asshole or anything. I just wanted to make sure you don't embarrass yourself. He still sounds like a really great guy."

"Thanks," I say. "I'll talk to you later, okay?"

"Okay, hon. Bye."

Chapter 15

Monday, November 7, 8:30 a.m., Sacramento

STEVE IS ON his way out the door to leave for work, and I've got Ella on my hip, sobbing. For some reason, she decided that today she was going to "be just like Daddy."

When Steve shaved, Ella wanted to shave too. Steve, ever indulgent, let her cover her baby-smooth cheeks with shaving cream and scrape it off with a plastic safety-capped razor. When Steve got dressed for work, Ella wanted to wear a tie too, so Steve tied an old one around her neck. Now crying, she has just wiped her snotty nose on it.

"I have to go to work too!" she's says. "I'm an arky-techt too."

"Of course you are, honey," Steve says, patting Ella's shoulder as he simultaneously glances at his watch. "How about if you design a house while Daddy's at work, and you can show me when I get home?"

Ella grabs his arm with a death grip.

"No, Daddy! Don't leave me!"

Steve whispers in my ear. "I'm late as shit. Can you handle her?"

"Just go," I say. "I'll deal with it."

Steve kisses Ella quickly, doesn't even say good-bye to me, and is out the door.

And the strange thing is, I don't even really mind. I've been kissing Tony so much lately that I don't feel very deprived. Ella's screams miraculously die down the second the door clicks behind Steve.

"Okay, my little master manipulator, let's give you a bath. You're sticky and snotty." I carry her up the stairs, noting that she's grown heavier lately.

As I draw a bath, flashes of Tony invade my mind. I remember when I used to be this preoccupied with Steve. It isn't as if I'm tired of him, of course. I still get a giddy feeling when he calls from work just to say hello. But lately, his hours seem to be getting later and later. With a bit of a shock, I realize that it's been nearly a month since we've had sex.

As I absentmindedly scrub Ella's back with a washcloth, I contemplate what to wear tomorrow for my date with Tony. Maybe I'll see if I can borrow something from Jana. She has an amazing wardrobe; she has to with all the auditions she goes on. I, on the other hand, won't have the cash for new clothes until I get my check from the Public. Just then, the telephone rings.

I look down at Ella in the tub. I know I shouldn't leave her alone, but she's a pretty big girl now, at three, and I'll be back in just a second. I duck into my bedroom, grab the portable phone, and am back in the bathroom before Ella has had a chance to notice I left.

Through the receiver, I can hear someone sobbing.

"Mom?"

"Angie," she says, gasping between sobs, "your dad has cancer."

"Oh my God. What kind?" I say, my brain in overdrive. *Please, God, let it be something curable, something they caught early. Let him be okay.*

"Lung."

"Shit," I say quietly. Ella stops playing with her bath toys and looks at me intently. "What stage?"

I'm answered by a sob. "Stage four. Angela, he's terminal. They gave him two months. Two fucking months. With chemo, it could be three to four. He won't do it though. He said no chemo. God, oh God..."

I feel the world literally drop out from under me. As if everything I knew to be safe and good was merely a deception. My world is ending as I know it. My daddy is going to die. I feel my chest tighten, and I actually watch the room spin. I sit down on the toilet seat. "Should I come over?"

"No," my mom says. "Come tomorrow. Your dad isn't ready to see anyone yet."

I click the phone off, and then, for the first time in front of Ella, I lose complete control. I'm shaking and screaming, and I know I'm scaring Ella, but it's as if I'm standing outside myself, watching. I just can't stop.

Ella's lip juts out, and she starts to cry too.

"Everything's okay, Ella," I hear myself say. Not even thinking, I scoop her up, naked, out of the tub and clutch her to me, as though she is the only solid thing left in the world. I call Steve. Within fifteen minutes, he rushes through the front door to find me sitting on the couch in a big puddle of water, sobbing, Ella still naked on my lap.

"Oh, sweetheart," Steve says. And he takes Ella and dresses her, and then he wraps me in a flannel blanket, like a child, and takes me to bed, where he just holds me while Ella watches the Disney Channel.

Monday, November 7, 2:25 p.m., New York

Here in my little Chelsea apartment, the fact that my dad is dying seems like only a bad dream. Right now, despite my domestic pleasures with Steve and Ella, I truly hope that my California life is a dream. *Let this life be the real one*, I beg silently. As I go about my business, painting a bit and then cleaning my kitchen, my mind keeps returning to my other life.

"He's terminal," my mom had said.

A glass, slippery with soap, falls to the ground and shatters, breaking into thousands of tiny shards.

"Fuck!" I start to cry. If my other life is truly an alternate version of this life, as I believe it is, then my dad here may very well have cancer too. I go straight to the phone and dial my parents' number. My mom answers.

"Hi, Mommy," I say in a small voice.

"Hi, dear," says my mom. "Are you okay?"

"Yeah. Um, I miss you guys. Can I come over for dinner?"

"Oh! Sure, sweetie, as long as you don't mind having leftovers. I'm not cooking tonight. I just went to the spa, and I feel so relaxed after my massage, I just can't imagine making dinner. But yeah, of course, we'd love to have you."

"Okay, I'll be over at six."

Then I call Tony and cancel our date. I tell him I feel like I'm coming down with something.

"Do you want me to bring you some chicken soup?" he says.

"No, please don't come over. I don't want to get you sick, and truthfully, I couldn't eat anything right now."

"Oh, okay, well, Saturday then?" he says, a hint of disappointment in his voice.

"Sure thing."

That night, I feel safe inside in my parents' upper-west-side three bedroom. My mom is in the too-small, yet large by New York standards, kitchen, reheating a pot roast, and I'm sitting on the couch with my dad, in front of a football game. It's the Bears versus the Falcons, and my dad is rooting for the Bears.

"So, how's that show going, honey?"

"Good…Dad? Have you had a physical lately, by any chance? Because you should be screened for stuff at your age. Colonoscopy, EKG, CT scan, you know…the works. Check for cancer…"

My dad pulls away from the screen and stares at me.

"Whoa there. I know I'm kind of old, but I'm perfectly healthy."

"Have you seen a doctor lately?"

He shakes his head. "I went for a physical three years ago, and I was fine. Don't worry." He pats my knee. "But thanks for looking out for your old man."

I help Mom set the table. "New china?" I look down at the white bowls with a brightly colored blossom painted inside each one.

"You like them?" She puts a spoon at each place.

"Yeah," I say. And then I whisper, "Mom, Dad needs to be checked for lung cancer. You have to make him go. Please."

My mom stops and looks at me searchingly, concern in her eyes.

"Angie, what has gotten into you? Your father is fine."

"No, Mom," I say, my heart beating wildly, "he's not!"

"Hey!" my dad says from the living room. "I'm not deaf, you know!"

I begin to get dizzy. I know they aren't going to listen to me.

"Dad, I just think you should have a body scan to make sure you don't have cancer."

My dad mutes the sound on the game.

"What is up with you today, Angela? Do you know something I don't?"

Before I can stop myself, the words tumble from my mouth.

"Look, I know you guys don't believe in my other life. I know you don't, but...okay, remember when I took the SATs and I got a perfect verbal score? I had spent hours memorizing vocabulary words, and you said, 'How do you know which words to study?' The thing is, I really did know which words to study because I had taken the test before. In California. I knew what was going to be on the test."

"Honey..."

"No, listen," I say to my dad. "I know it seems crazy to you, but...my dad in California just got diagnosed with lung cancer and was only given two months to live."

"It was just a dream, dear," my mom says. "Your dad feels fine."

"Which is why he needs to get checked now, before it's too late. He might not even have cancer. Lots of things are different here than they are there. But I think it's important to find out for sure."

My mom spoons some pot roast into my dish and purses her lips. "Honey, I know that your dreams are very vivid..." She trails off when she sees the look on my face. "Angela, are you still seeing a therapist?"

"No! I'm tired of seeing these patronizing doctors who just want to keep me medicated."

My mom puts her hand on mine. "These CT scans give a ton of radiation. I read in the *Times* that it's something comparable to the radiation of being near a nuclear war zone. They don't recommend it without a medical indication."

I pull my hand away. "By the time you have symptoms, it's too late!" I turn to my dad. "Please, Daddy. I don't want to lose you too."

My dad shakes his head. "You won't. I'm fine. You can't let yourself get so worked up about it."

I look at my dad, and suddenly I'm blinded by tears. I run out the door.

Chapter 16

"Hi, Grandma, it's Angie," I said.

"Oh, Angie, hello, dear." My grandmother's voice was gravelly from years of smoking. "How are you?"

"Fine." I opened a piece of watermelon-flavored Bubbalicious gum and put it in my mouth. "I have to research my family history for my class. I'm just calling to see if you can help me fill in my family tree."

"Of course. What do you need to know?"

I recited the categories to my grandma, and she gave me names and birthdates, which I dutifully recorded. I fanned myself with my hand. It was hot in the house. My bare legs were sticking to the shiny wooden chair at the kitchen table. I snapped my gum as I wrote, my handwriting tiny but legible.

"Your father's information," I requested.

"Oh, his name was George Myers. And his birthday was September 12, 1910."

After about half an hour, I had all the information my grandma could remember. I felt warm inside, talking to her, and I missed her because she lived in New York. In my life there, I saw her all the time, but in this life, only every few years. She was almost exactly the same there, but I still missed *this* grandma. She was the only one who would read my stories and tell me they were as good as a real book. For some reason, I didn't write stories in New York. I tried, but they never came out any good. And here, I never really drew or painted. I just wasn't very interested. Strange...yet another one of the mysteries of my life.

"Thanks, Grandma," I said. "I'll see you at Christmas."

"Okay, dear. You be good for your mom. Love you."

"Love you."

That night, in bed, I stared at the space next to my pillow, trying to find shapes in the textured drywall. Something was nagging at me, but I couldn't put my finger on what it was. I had this feeling that I did something incorrectly. I mentally went over my math equations. No, all of the long division checked out perfectly. I know I did my vocabulary words right, because my mom had checked them. My eyes fell on a certain shape on the wall that looked like an angel blowing a horn. The angel Gabriel…Gabriel, that was it! My grandma had told me that her father's name was George, but I remembered very clearly that his name was Gabriel. Gabriel Thomas, I believe. Yes. My grandmother in my other life had a huge picture of her parents up in the living room, their wedding picture, and beneath it was their names: Mr. and Mrs. Gabriel Thomas.

This didn't make any sense. It wasn't one of those things that could be different in my different lives, like my artistic abilities. No, if my grandma here had a different father than my grandma there, she wouldn't be the exact same person. And if she wasn't the same person, then my mom couldn't exist, and if my mom couldn't exist, neither could I. I practically jumped out of bed and ran into my mom's room.

"Mom!" I said.

She looked up from her sewing. "What, honey? I thought you were asleep."

I shook my head and sat down on the bed beside her, my red flannel nightgown twisting around my legs. "Mom, what was your grandfather's name? Was it Gabriel or George?"

"George. Didn't you just get this information from Grandma?"

"Yes." I picked up a spool of green thread and rolled it around in my hand. "But I thought it was Gabriel Thomas. Remember, because Grandma's name was Louise Thomas before she married Grandpa."

My mom gives me a funny look. "Honey, I don't know what you're thinking of, but my grandpa was definitely named George. And Grandma's name was Louise Myers."

I unwound a bit of thread and wrinkled my brow. I wanted desperately to explain to my mom why I was so confused. I wanted her to understand and to have the perfect answer, just like she usually did. But I knew that if I brought up my life in New York, she wouldn't understand at all. She would just tell me it was a dream and make me go back to the doctor. And worst of all, she would have that sad look in her eyes. I dreaded seeing that look. Because I knew it pained her terribly to think that her daughter was crazy. And that's exactly what she would think if I let her know even a fraction of the things I thought.

"Why don't you scoot off to bed, Angie? You look tired."

"Okay," I said. I could feel a lump building in my throat, but I swallowed hard and went back to my bedroom. I was ten years old, and it was time to stop being a baby. I would have to solve this mystery on my own.

I reached under my bed for my Super Secret Detective Kit. I had put this kit together myself. There was a baggie of chalk for dusting for fingerprints, a hand-held tape recorder for suspect interviews, and a flashlight for nighttime crime solving. So far, I hadn't used any of it. But now I had a real mystery to solve. I didn't know how the kit would help me solve this particular family mystery, but I had a hunch it would come in handy somehow.

Chapter 17

Tuesday, November 15, 3:20 p.m., Sacramento

My dad's goal is to make it until January. He says that he doesn't want us to have a sad Christmas. As if it won't be sad anyway. But the chance to spend one last Christmas with him is one that means a lot to us all.

Today, just as I have every day this week, I pick Ella up from preschool, and we go over to my parents' house and visit my dad. In a way, I do feel blessed that we are being allowed to have a long good-bye. But on the other hand, it is gut wrenching to know that we have so little time left.

As Ella and I are walking up the driveway, I realize that she has started to cry.

"What's wrong, little bear?" I say, kneeling down at her level.

"I don't want Grandpa to go to heaven," she says, sniffling. "I want him to take me to the Ice Capades instead."

"I know." I hug her, tears welling up in my own eyes. "I wish he could stay here too. But he'll be so happy up in heaven, and then one day a long, long time from now, we'll go to heaven too, and we'll all be together again."

She considers this idea. "And we'll have white, not purple, wings?"

"You can have whatever color you want." I kiss her forehead in that sweet spot where her hairline begins, all fuzzy and soft. Then I pick her up and head into the house.

"Hi, sweetie," my mom says, scooping Ella out of my arms. "Who wants chocolate-chip cookies?"

"I do!" says Ella.

I squeeze my mom's shoulder. "How are you feeling?"

She shakes her head, and I see that she can't speak, or she will start to cry. Nevertheless, she forces her lips into a smile. "Let's go have some cookies!" she says as she carries Ella into the kitchen.

My dad is sitting on the couch. He shifts in his seat and winces. I know that he must be in pain.

"Are you okay, Dad?"

"Take your pain pill, Tom," my mom calls from the kitchen.

"Here," I say, opening the orange bottle on the coffee table and handing him a pill. "Let me get you a glass of water."

But before I can leave the room, my mom has come in with a glass of water. I see that she already has Ella sitting on a booster chair at the table, with a plate of cookies and a glass of milk in front of her.

"Angie, did your dad tell you about what they did at UC Davis for him?"

I shake my head.

"Tell her, Tom." My mom sits down on the arm of the couch.

His eyes look a bit wet. "They had a tribute for me. All the faculty and…and the students from all these years. I mean…so many of them came, Angela. And people spoke."

My mom nods. "Oh, Angie, it was so wonderful. These kids, they kept saying how your father is their hero, how he is their inspiration. One woman came all the way from Florida. It was really beautiful. And then all your father's friends, his colleagues, they all had the most kind things to say as well. A lot of them have been coming by too. Saying their good-byes." Her voice catches, and she squeezes my dad's hand.

"Dad, how are you doing?" I say.

"Not so hot, honey. I know I'm an old guy, but having you kids so late always made me feel younger than I was, you know?"

"Yeah. You always seemed younger too."

I can't believe how brave he's being, sitting here calmly discussing his own death. In a way, it's unnerving. But it also makes it easier. We don't have to pretend that everything is going to be all right.

"Angie, I've been thinking," he says. "What if that dream life of yours turned out to be a parallel universe after all?"

"Are you serious?" I say. "After all that money you spent on psychiatrists?"

"No, I know, but it's just…if there is a parallel universe, then when I die…I don't completely stop existing, do I?"

"I don't know, Dad," I say, playing with the fringe on my blouse. "The you that exists over there isn't getting tested. I'm really scared that he has cancer too."

"Well, sweetie, you tell him he better find out. Tell him I said he's a lousy piece of shit if he doesn't." He looks surprised at his own outburst. "If nothing else, maybe it will save you a really bad dream."

Thursday, November 24, 12:36 p.m., Sacramento

Steve, Ella, and I are at my parents' house for Thanksgiving. It was supposed to be our year with Steve's parents, but obviously, the plans had to be changed. My mom has put all of her pain and rage into her cooking and cleaning, so the house looks beautiful, and there is a feast like we've never had before. I could almost pretend that everything was going to be okay.

The doorbell rings as everyone is eating crackers and cheese. I answer the door. It is my older brother, Jonathan. In the vestibule, he hugs me.

"Hey, little sister!" He smiles, but I can see that his eyes are red from crying in the car on the way down from Seattle, where he and his wife, Janine, run a T-shirt printing business.

"Where's Janine?" I say, looking behind him.

"Well, uh, here's the thing." Jonathan pulls me out onto the porch and closes the door behind us. "Janine and I are separated. I have a new girlfriend…and so does Janine."

"Oh, Jonathan, I'm so sorry."

"No, it's fine. Really. I wish she had figured out that she was a lesbian before we got married, but better now than ten years down the road, with three kids and a mortgage, right?"

"Why didn't you tell us?" I say. "When did this all happen?"

"Right around when Dad was getting sick. I'm sorry I didn't tell you sooner, but I just didn't want anyone to worry about me right now. Anyway, I'm okay. I'm seeing this real sweet girl, having a good time. Don't worry about it."

Wow. I am stunned. Janine and Jonathan had seemed really happy together. Not only am I surprised that she left him, I'm surprised he's taking it so well.

"Are you gonna tell Dad and Mom?" I say. I know my mom is not going to take this well.

"Yeah, I'll tell them tomorrow probably. I don't want to mess up Thanksgiving more than it's already messed up. I'm gonna say Janine is sick."

"How are you doing?" I say, touching his arm.

A tear escapes from the corner of his eye. "Pretty damn shitty, actually. You?"

"I'm doing pretty damn shitty myself. Thanks for asking. Wanna come inside?"

Thanksgiving ends up being as nice as could possibly be expected, considering the circumstances. It is nice to have the whole family together. For this one day, no one really talks about the cancer. My dad actually has a good appetite, which I'm grateful for. I really wanted him to enjoy his last Thanksgiving.

"At least it doesn't matter if I get fat now!" he says as he takes a third piece of pie.

My mom looks tired. I can't imagine how hard it must be for her to put on a brave face right now.

After dinner, we play a family game of Scrabble, a cherished Thanksgiving tradition. We play as partners. My dad and I are a team. We win. Of course, we've won every year for the last ten years. For the first time though, no one cares.

Later, my parents go to bed, and Steve volunteers to put Ella down as well.

Jonathan and I remain downstairs. "Do you want to watch a movie?" Jonathan says.

"No…all I feel like doing is getting drunk."

"I hear ya. We could both use a drink." Jonathan gets several bottles of alcohol out of my parents' liquor cabinet. "What are you having? Gin and tonic? Rum and Coke?"

"Rum and Coke."

I'm glad my brother is home. It makes everything seem so much more normal. We joke and chat, and by the time we move on to our second drink, Steve has come downstairs. Jonathan pours him a drink, and we all go sit on the couch together. I lean back against the cushion.

"So tell me about this girl you're seeing," says Steve.

Jonathan looks at me questioningly.

"I told him. You don't mind, do you?" I say.

"No, it's fine," Jonathan says. He turns toward Steve. "Her name's Katie, and she's really cool. It's pretty casual right now, but I like her."

Steve nods. "Good, glad to hear that. Sorry about Janine."

Jonathan shakes his head. "Yeah, me too." He lowers his voice. "Oh, but I didn't even tell you the best part. Guess what Janine's girlfriend's name is? Amber *Topaz*."

"Oh shut up!" I say, laughing. "No it's not!"

"It is. I swear I'm not making this up. Apparently she's some kind of alternative healer or something. She's pretty hot actually. I'd leave me for her too... Anyway, Katie's pretty smokin' herself. Her body is incredible—"

I cringe. "Please. Spare me the details."

"So how are you guys holding up, really?" Jonathan asks, taking a sip of his drink.

Steve sighs. "Man, this is really hard. I never expected we'd be dealing with this now. Maybe when Ella was in college or something. I know he's older, but I guess I just didn't think about it."

Jonathan takes a drag of his cigarette. "Yeah. I know. I didn't think I'd lose my dad before I even had my own kids. At least he got to meet Elly, you know?"

I feel a wave of sadness wash over me. "I can't believe we only have another month with Dad," I say.

"Yeah, Ang, what the hell is up with that?" Jonathan says, hitting his forehead. "What is this with Dad not doing chemo? Don't you think he should be doing chemo?"

"I don't know," I say. "The thing is, the doctor said that at this point the chemo would only prolong his life by a few months. He would have to have all those trips to the doctor, all the side effects. He just isn't into it."

"Yeah, but what about us? Maybe we want him around for a few more months."

"I know." I shake my head. "But it's Dad's choice. Dad just wants to be here at home, not in a hospital. He wants to die here with his family."

"God, this sucks!" Jonathan says, standing up. He paces around the room. "This sucks! It fucking, fucking sucks!" He starts to cry.

"I know," I say, and I can't hold back my own tears.

He looks at me. "Why, Angie? Why Dad? He's a good person. He doesn't deserve this."

I stand up and hug my brother, both of us sobbing. Steve sits on the couch, powerless to help either one of us and knowing it.

Thursday, November 24, 5:35 p.m., New York

When I told my dad that his California doppelgänger said he was being a piece of shit, he went silent. I knew from experience that this was not a good sign. So despite my desire to bring Tony to my parents' home for Thanksgiving, I have agreed to go with him to Vermont instead, and we are now on the road, headed for a romantic weekend getaway.

I can't help thinking that if Tony and I end up together, this is the first of many Thanksgivings we will share. And it feels freeing to be out in the beautiful countryside, surrounded by the most incredible foliage, in the crisp November air. I feel myself slowly relax.

"What are you thinking about?" Tony says, putting his hand on my leg.

"Oh, nothing...Actually, I'm just thinking about my family. I miss them. But I'm happy to be here with you," I say.

He looks wistful. "I miss my family too. Hopefully, I'll get out to Greece next summer at some point. We'll see."

Somehow, I get the feeling that he is sizing me up. I have a feeling that he is thinking about inviting me to go with him.

We pull up to the bed and breakfast, and it looks like a cottage out of a fairy tale. There is even an apple orchard in the back with a hand-painted wooden sign saying "All you can pick apples." Tony drives down the unpaved driveway that leads to a parking area around the side. As we step out of the car, a golden retriever greets us. We walk up the stone walkway to the house and find that inside, it is even more picturesque. The house smells of apples and is decorated with a mixture of Amish-style furniture, country antiques, and homemade crafts. A woman emerges from the kitchen, holding the fattest white cat I've ever seen. She introduces herself as "Gran" and takes us up the wooden staircase to a sweet little room with an overstuffed couch, a four-poster bed, and a handmade desk and chair. A heart-shaped wooden plaque above the bed reads Welcome Home.

I thrill a little, thinking that this is my first trip with Tony. A milestone. In my green leather bag I've packed a toothbrush, a few outfits, and a brand-new red lace teddy with a garter belt.

That night, Tony and I are ensconced in the booth of a tiny little restaurant, dim and candlelit, enjoying sweet potatoes, turkey, and green beans, when my cell phone rings. I see from the caller ID that it's my parents.

"I'll be right back," I say to Tony, heading outside in front of the restaurant. Over the course of the day, it has turned considerably colder. A few flakes of snow are beginning to fall, and the silence is almost audible.

"Hello?" I say, putting the phone to my ear.

"Hi, honey," my dad says. "Happy Thanksgiving. We wish you were here."

"Happy Thanksgiving," I say weakly.

"Look, Angie, I'm sorry, okay? I feel bad about how upset you've been, and frankly, you've got me a little creeped out as well, so tomorrow I'm going to call my doctor and see if I can get an appointment."

"Thank you, Daddy!" Relief floods my body. I can see my breath in the air, and I shiver, wishing I had remembered to grab my coat on the way out. "Sorry I called you a shit," I say.

"Oh, that's okay." He laughs. "Anyway, your mom says to ask you if you'll come have some Thanksgiving leftovers with us next week. Anyway, we all miss you, and we love you."

"I love you too, Dad," I say, my teeth chattering. "Tell everyone I love them and I'll be over in a few days when I get back from Vermont."

"Sure thing. Oh, and guess what? We tried doing that blackened turkey thing your mom saw on Pinterest, and now the whole house smells like ass. But we have the best damned turkey you've ever had."

I chuckle to myself as I head back into the restaurant.

Now I feel that now I can actually enjoy Thanksgiving. But another part of me feels a gnawing fear in the pit of my stomach. Soon, I'll find out. And I might end up losing my dad twice.

Sunday, November 27, 10:32 a.m., Sacramento

I come downstairs in my parents' house and pour myself some coffee. My dad is sitting at the table with a bowl of cereal and the *Sacramento Bee.* Next to his bowl is a plate of Jonathan's "special brownies."

I raise my eyebrows. "So I guess you confiscated Jonathan's stash?"

"Nah," he says, grinning. "He gave them to his old man before he left this morning. He's a good kid."

Chapter 18

Monday, December 5, 8:19 p.m., New York

Tony and I are watching Netflix in bed, munching popcorn and eating raw cookie dough.

The phone rings, and I groan, putting the movie on pause and grabbing the receiver.

"Hello?"

I hear sobbing on the other end of the line. And I know beyond a shadow of a doubt that the news is not good. I can't live through this conversation again. I just can't.

"Mom?" I say

"Daddy has cancer," she says. "There's a tumor in his lungs."

Tony looks at me with concern in his eyes.

"Is he terminal?" I say, a lump building in my throat.

My mom sobs, and my knees give out from under me.

"No, honey. We didn't want to tell you until we knew for sure. But the doctor just called and he said it's only stage one. They are going to do surgery and chemo, and the doctor said there is a good prognosis. They think they caught it in time. The doctor said that by the time he showed symptoms, it would probably have been too late. And he never would have had the scan if it wasn't for you. You saved Daddy's life. Oh, Angela, I'm so sorry. You were right. You were right."

I am still shaking, but now I feel a happiness I haven't felt in weeks. "I'm just glad they caught it, Mom. I love you, okay?"

"Angie, what's going on? What happened?" Tony asks.

Tears of happiness pour down my cheeks. "My dad has lung cancer. But they think they caught it in time."

He wipes the tears from my cheeks with his sleeve. "Don't cry, baby. It's all going to be okay. Your dad will be fine."

I nestle into his arms. "I love you," I say.

"Come here, sweetie." He pulls me into a spoon position on the bed. It is only later, after he has gone home, that I realize he never said "I love you too."

Thursday, December 15, 4:25 p.m., New York

My mother, my brother, Jonathan, and I are gathered around my father. He is about to go into surgery to have the tumor removed from his lungs. I am sitting on a chair by the hospital bed, holding his hand.

"Are you scared, Daddy?" I say.

"Well," he says matter of factly, "either I'll wake up tomorrow or I won't."

"Dad…" Jonathan says.

"For God's sake, Tom," my mom says. "Don't talk like that. You'll be fine. You're a healthy man. Except for the cancer. But you'll be okay. You have to be."

We all hug him and then go into the lobby to wait.

Periodically, a doctor comes out and updates us. My mom is so nervous she can't sit down. She just keeps pacing around the room, which makes me even more nervous. Jonathan deals with the situation by eating. I watch in disgust as he devours countless peanut butter and orange crackers from the vending machine. All I can do is sit, reading the same *Marie Claire* article over and over because I can't get the words to make sense.

Finally, the doctor comes out with a big smile on his face. Thank God.

"Well, guys, he did great. We got the entire tumor out, and we didn't have to take too much healthy tissue. You can see him when he wakes up, and then in a few days he'll be able to go home. When he recovers a little bit, we'll start the chemo."

I hug my mom, both of us crying. Even Jonathan's eyes are full of tears. My dad is going to be okay. He isn't going to die.

Chapter 19

THE NEXT DAY at school, Dan avoided me. He wasn't waiting for me at my locker. He wasn't standing outside my geometry class to walk me to French. He wasn't even in the usual spot we met for lunch. I felt panic rise in my chest. Was he going to break up with me? It wasn't possible. We were engaged. I looked down at the ring on my finger. I was his, and he loved me. He wouldn't break up with me the day after he proposed. The day after I gave him my virginity.

I searched the cafeteria, looking for his familiar black clothes, but all I saw were throngs of other students, each clique at a separate table: the cheerleaders, the jocks, the goths, the nerds...but no Dan. Finally, I gave up and headed toward the library. No way was I going to eat lunch alone like a loser. I might as well use the time to do a little homework.

I stepped inside the library, and the comforting musty smell of books made me feel slightly better. The cool air-conditioned breeze in this newer wing of the building made my skin stand up in goose bumps. I headed toward the biography section. I was supposed to research Van Gogh for my art history class. I ran my hand over the spines of the books. Some of them were really old and starting to fall apart. Others were brand new and full of color pictures, usually donated in someone's name to the school. I pulled out one of these new books and began to leaf through the pages.

And then I heard Dan's voice. He was laughing. I peeked through the stack, and I saw that, off in an armchair in the corner, Dan was sitting next to my best friend, Brie, and they were looking at a magazine together. Why would they ditch me like that? I felt betrayed, but I knew there was probably a logical explanation. I walked toward them, and as I did, they both looked up. Dan didn't stand up to hug me, and he didn't pull me down onto his lap. Something was definitely not right.

"Hey, what are you guys doing?" I said.

"Oh, nothing," Dan said. "Just hanging out. It was too hot in the cafeteria."

"Where were you earlier?" I said.

Dan shrugged. "I wasn't in the mood for school. I ditched."

"Oh, okay."

I looked at Brie, but she didn't meet my eye. And then I knew, without a doubt, that Dan had told her what happened yesterday. Tears of shame prickled behind my eyelids. How could he do that to me? How could he share the most intimate details of our sex life with anyone else?

"Dan, can we go somewhere and talk?" I said in a falsely cheerful voice.

He sighed, clearly understanding that this talk wasn't going to be much fun. "Okay." He stood and followed me to the back of the library, where no one could overhear us.

"What's up?" he said.

I bit my lip. "Dan, it's kind of obvious that you're avoiding me. Are you really freaked out about what happened yesterday? Maybe we should talk about it."

"I *don't* want to talk about it," he said. "I'd rather just try to forget about it." He shuddered.

"I feel like you're mad at me or something. You know it wasn't my fault. I'm sorry about your sheets. I just...I don't know what you thought was going to happen."

"Of course it wasn't your fault. I'm not mad...Let's just pretend it never happened."

"Fine with me," I said. "But are we okay? Are we still engaged?"

"Of course, Angela," he said. But his tone sounded dismissive. "Everything's completely fine between us."

I nodded, desperate to believe him. "So why did you tell Brie what happened?"

His eyes widened. "What?"

"I know you told her," I said. "I could tell."

He sighed. "Yeah, okay, but I knew you were going to tell her anyway. I was just a little freaked, that's all."

I didn't know what to say. He was right. I was planning to tell her. But it still seemed like such a betrayal. Still, I didn't want to cause any more problems than we already had.

"Okay, so do you want to ditch fifth period with me?" I said.

"And have sex again?"

"Well, no," I said. "I think I need to recover a little first."

"So there isn't really any point, then."

No point? "Well, couldn't we just kiss?" I said.

He shrugged, and I wanted to punch him.

"Now that we've had sex, kissing would be too frustrating."

"Well, couldn't we just hang out?" I whispered.

"Mmm, I don't know. I actually shouldn't skip fifth period today. I already ditched the whole morning."

What was going on? Dan never passed up an opportunity to miss class. I blinked back tears.

"Okay," I said. "But you still love me, right?" I leaned in for a kiss.

Dan gave me a quick hug and a peck on the cheek. I couldn't remember him ever kissing me on the cheek.

"Sure," he said.

As I walked to the train after school, I wondered if everything would be all right with Dan. He said he still loved me. But then why was he acting so weird? I desperately wanted to talk to my mom. I knew she would know what to do. But how could I talk to her about this? And even if I could, she would probably tell my dad, and then I'd never be allowed to leave the house again. What had I gotten myself into? I never should have slept with Dan. I tried to quell the panic I felt building in my stomach. It would be okay; things might be strange for a few days, but Dan would get over it soon. And then everything would go back to normal.

That night, Dan didn't call me. And I didn't call him. I decided to wait it out. I did call Brie, but she didn't answer. Finally, I went to bed, hoping that tomorrow it would all be okay.

But it wasn't. When I arrived at school, I noticed something strange. Whenever I walked past people I knew, they looked away. Or whispered to each other. And there was only one explanation: Brie had told everyone I had slept with Dan. I knew she loved to gossip, but about me? No wonder she didn't answer her phone all night. How could she do that to me? I wanted to fold myself up into a ball and hide in my locker. *Everyone* knew. I was so angry that I was shaking.

I practically ran toward the science rooms, hoping to intercept Brie before her biology class. But as I rounded the corner, I saw something that made me stop in my tracks. She was standing right next to the door of the classroom. And there behind her, his arms hooked around her, just below her breasts, was Dan. They didn't see me, but I could see them clearly. Then Dan leaned forward and kissed Brie on the neck. My stomach heaved. Dan was cheating on me with my best friend!

I swallowed the bile rising in my throat and walked toward them. "What's going on?" I said, nearly shouting.

Brie looked at the ground, but Dan looked me right in the eye.

"Sorry, Angie. It's not really going to work out with us. I think Brie and I are more compatible."

Hot tears flooded my eyes. I noticed that a crowd of students had gathered to watch the altercation…To witness my humiliation. Well, let them watch. I had no more shame now.

"More *sexually* compatible," I said. "Let's just be clear. And by the way, usually you dump the person you're engaged to before you get a new girlfriend."

I looked at the ring on my finger, my "engagement" ring, and I realized with a stab of embarrassment that it had only ever been a sham, just a way to convince me to sleep with him. Suddenly, the ring looked cheap, hideous. How could I have ever been so stupid? I pulled the ring from my finger and threw it at him. It bounced off his leather jacket and fell on the hardwood floor with a clang.

"Enjoy your sloppy seconds," I said to Brie as tears clouded my vision.

And then I ran all the way to the subway. I didn't know where I was going, but I knew I had to get away from that school.

Chapter 20

Wednesday, December 27, 5:31 p.m., Sacramento

My dad made it through Christmas. It was the worst nightmare of a Christmas I ever lived through. He was like a shell of his former self. Since Thanksgiving, his appetite had declined. As a result of that and his cancer depriving his healthy cells of nutrients, he had lost thirty pounds.

Thankfully, he wasn't in a great deal of pain. He was taking large amounts of morphine and was largely out of it. There seemed to be little point in giving him gifts, but we gave him things to try to brighten his spirits. A warm fuzzy sweater, soft socks, a blanket. And we wrote him a letter telling him how much he meant to us. He cried when we read it to him.

Now I'm sitting next to the hospital bed my mom has set up in the living room, and holding his hand. None of us can believe how fast he's declined. Faster than even the doctors had predicted. But Dad said he just wanted to say his good-byes, have one last Christmas, and get out of here. He didn't want to linger.

Ella is sitting on my lap, rubbing my dad's forehead—"Petting him," she says. I can see that he is touched.

"Angie," he says, "make sure this little girl doesn't forget me."

"I will." A tear rolls down my cheek.

My mom walks up and puts her hand on my shoulder. "Do you want me to give Ella a bath?" she says.

I glance at Steve, on the couch, but he has fallen asleep. He's been so tired lately, poor guy.

"Sure," I say, lifting Ella and putting her into my mother's arms.

I watch my mom take Ella upstairs. I can hear her singing softly.

I squeeze my dad's hand, but he doesn't squeeze back. His pulse is weak.

"I love you," he whispers, almost inaudibly.

"I love you too," I say, kissing his forehead. "Dad?"

He doesn't answer me. "Daddy?" I say again in a small voice. And then I know that he is gone. I lay my head on his chest, like a little girl, and cry.

Wednesday, December 27, 11:02 a.m., New York

I wake up in my little single bed in my parents' apartment and run into the kitchen, crying.

"Honey, what's the matter?" says my mom, her voice full of concern.

"Daddy died," I say. "He died." And my mom holds me in her arms while I sob.

My dad looks up from his paper.

"I died?"

I turn to him. "Yeah, you did."

He shakes his head, bewildered. "You saved my life, little girl. You saved my life."

Saturday, December 30, 1:30 p.m., Sacramento

My father's funeral is the most surreal event I have ever experienced. Our car pulls into the church parking lot, and I see the throngs of people in black heading into the church. Steve squeezes my hand as he parks the car.

"Okay, Angie, you and Ella go sit up in front with your mom. I'll join you after we bring in the casket. Are you going to be okay going in alone?" he says, kissing my forehead.

I nod. Since Wednesday, I have been unable to shed a tear. It is as though I already cried out all the tears I had in me. Now I just feel like a hollow shell, going through the motions but feeling nothing. I gave all I had to give. Holding Ella on my hip, I walk into the church, hardly noticing the people who offer me condolences.

The minister walks to the front and says a few words. Then Steve, Jonathan, Steve's dad, and my uncle Rob carry in the casket. It comforts me to see these four men, youthful and strong, bearing my father in. My mom starts to cry as soon as she sees them, but I don't feel any emotion. I only realize with a kind of horror as I look at the pallbearers that I will almost certainly one day attend some of their funerals. I shake my head and smooth Ella's bangs. She tilts her head at me.

"It's okay, Mommy," she says, patting my arm. "Don't be scared."

I kiss her chubby cheek. Soon, Steve is beside me. The service passes in a blur. People cry. My uncle sings. The minister talks. I read the letter we wrote my dad for Christmas, without really understanding what I am reading. It is an open casket, and we have a chance to view the body. When I walk up and see my father lying there, I just can't comprehend that he is no longer alive. He looks as though he has just gone to sleep. I know this is probably due to the magic of the mortician, but just the same, he looks so alive, so handsome in his suit, without any pain marring his features. Without thinking, I reach out and touch his hand. I shudder. He is cold and pasty. *This isn't my dad. He's already gone.*

At the cemetery, I put a rose on my father's casket.

"Good-bye, Daddy," I say.

Ella hugs my legs.

"Mommy, he's not in there. He's in heaven."

My mother shakes her head. "Would you listen to that." She turns to Ella. "That's right, honey. Grandpa is in heaven now."

In this moment, I almost wish I was three years old and that I could digest the idea of death with as little trouble as Ella does. The truth is, even with my father's body buried in the ground, cold and clammy, and his spirit surely somewhere else, I keep expecting to turn and see him come walking down the street, late because he overslept. My brain just refuses to believe he is dead. It is simply too terrible an idea to understand. But whether my brain comprehends it or not, I won't ever see him again. Of course, I'll see my father in New York, and for that I am eternally grateful. No one else in the world really has that chance, at least as far as I know. But my dad here was still a different person. The same, but subtly different. The experiences he had, the people he knew, all of those things shaped his personality. And he was the only father I had who shared the experiences of my life here in California, who knew this part of me. And he's the only one who knew Ella and got to be her grandfather.

At the reception at my parents' house, I am shocked to realize just how many people came to pay their respects to my dad. I recognize work colleagues, neighbors, all sorts of distant family members, friends of his from college, friends from high school, and numerous young people who I assume must be students of his. There is an abundance of food. Casseroles, muffins, noodles, fruit…And somehow, I am starving. But I don't even really taste the food when I eat it.

I walk into the backyard to find Ella and my cousin's son, Riley, playing catch and talking. Riley is four.

"You know your Grandpa died," Riley says to Ella matter of factly.

"Yeah, I know," says Ella. "He moved to heaven."

"Maybe next time when you come visit me in an airplane, you can visit your grandpa up in heaven too."

Ella looks at him like he's stupid. "You can't visit heaven, Riley. Not till you die." She looks thoughtful. "But I can talk to him whenever I want." Looking up at the sky, she begins to shout. "Hi, Grandpa. I love you! You missed good cake!"

Later, Steve takes Ella home, and I stay at my mom's house with Jonathan. That evening, we all gather in the kitchen. My mom serves us huge slices of chocolate fudge cake.

"Angie?" my mom says, taking a sip of milk. "You know how you used to talk about your life in New York?"

I'm extremely surprised that my mom is bringing this up. For the most part, I haven't talked about it since high school. I was so tired of having people think I was crazy—I just started keeping it to myself.

I nod at my mom, wondering where she is going with this.

"Well, I was just wondering. Did your dad there…I mean, did he pass also? Do you have to do this all again tomorrow?"

"No," I say. "Do you guys really want to hear about this?"

They both look at me eagerly.

"Okay. Well, actually…after Dad got diagnosed with cancer, I convinced my dad in New York to get tested. And it turned out that he did have cancer, but for some reason it hadn't spread yet, so they were able to do surgery and chemo, and they think he's going to be okay."

"Wow." Jonathan shakes his head. "So basically, if this other life of yours actually does exist, if it's not some crazy dream but actually is some kind of other reality or temporal flex or science fiction—whatever—then Dad is still out there somewhere, alive."

"Sort of," I reply. "The dad we grew up with here, he's dead. But there is, I'd say, another *version* of him living in New York."

"And some other version of you and me and mom are there with him?" he asks.

"Yep." I push the icing around on my plate. "And you live in Connecticut, and you work for a publicity firm in Manhattan. And you make an assload of money, which you use to take out a steady succession of really hot women. But recently, you started dating an artist who, while really beautiful, is also really smart, and I wish you would end up with her because I like her a lot." I turn to my mom. "And you volunteer for a bunch of organizations, although you took time off to help Dad with his surgery."

"Of course I did," she says, nodding approvingly.

"And I work as a costume designer, and I'm dating a superhot Greek writer named Tony."

"So...you're cheating on Steve?" says Jonathan.

"I'm not cheating on him!" I say, more harshly than I intended. "I am not married to Steve in that life, so I can do whatever I want."

My mom looks serious. "Angela?"

"Yeah, Mom?"

"Do you think...well, I mean...this might seem really weird, but could you tell your dad—I mean your dad there—well, could you tell him that I love him so much and that I really miss him?"

"Sure," I say, blinking back tears.

Chapter 21

Saturday, December 30, 8:34 p.m., New York

Ever since my dad had his surgery, I have been staying here with my parents in New York. Every day, when I return from a day of mourning in Sacramento, I am able to find peace and comfort by spending as much time as possible with my father here, especially since he is not working, but is home, doing chemo treatments and recovering from his surgery.

We spend a lot of the day together, watching movies, going for walks when he feels well enough, playing Scrabble. He seems to really appreciate the fact that I have pretty much dropped my life to help him through this hard time.

After tech week at the Public, I didn't take on another project. I have enough money saved to pay a month's rent, and I don't really have to pay for food, because I'm staying in my old room at my parents' apartment. My mom has turned it into her "dressing room," but my bed is still in there, so that's fine with me. I still go out with Tony every Friday night, but that's been it. I know he is feeling kind of neglected, but things have been a little weird ever since I told him I loved him and he didn't respond. I am hoping that he saw I was in the middle of a lot of emotion and that the words just came out. I am hoping that he loves me too and that he's just afraid to say it. But now, I just need to focus on my family. He seems to understand. He met my parents the first time he came to pick me up for a date.

My mom gushed about him.

"Oh, Angie," she said to me the next morning. "He is so handsome! And so polite and smart. I read some of those poems in his book. Is this guy even for real? And he is really into you—I can tell."

Jonathan was also there that night, but all he had to say was, "Meh."

Tonight, my parents and I are playing a game of Trivial Pursuit.

"Yes, another wedge for me!" my dad says triumphantly. He is beating me and Mom pretty badly, but I don't mind. I roll the dice but don't move my piece. My mind is in my other life.

"You okay, Ang?" my dad says.

"Dad…I went to your funeral."

He sighs. "That's a downer. Sorry, honey. I really am. I'm glad you get to be with me here though, right?"

"Well, yes," I say. "But the thing is, Mom and Jonathan, they're pretty upset. Because they don't get to see you ever again. And they aren't sure they believe in you exactly, but I think they really want to. And they said…they just wanted you to know that they really love you and that they miss you a lot."

"Wow." My dad's eyes fill with tears. "Honey, I'm not sure I believe in them either. But tell them that I wish I could be with them right now and that I'm thinking about them a lot. And that I love them more than anything."

My mother sighs. "It's so weird, Angie. In the back of my mind, I always wondered if maybe there was something to this 'other life' of yours. I mean, the kind of detailed things you would tell me, even at a young age. It was hard to believe you were just dreaming. But I didn't want to go against the doctors. I still don't really know what to think. But after your prediction about Dad's cancer, I just…I don't know. I…I've been thinking a lot about it. And, Angie, I'm sorry. I'm sorry that we made you feel crazy all of these years."

I can't believe it. I have waited to hear my mother say these words for my entire life. I feel hot tears behind my eyes. "Thank you," I whisper.

Tuesday, January 3, 7:45 p.m., New York

Tony and I are having dinner at Rosa Mexicano. For New York, the restaurant is massive, the walls dripping with waterfalls lit with pink and green lights.

We sit side by side in a cozy booth and sip delicious and very strong pomegranate margaritas, as a server makes fresh guacamole on a cart next to our table, to be served with warm tortilla chips. I can already feel myself getting a bit tipsy, which is alarming considering that I've only drunk about an eighth of the margarita.

Tony puts his arm around me as the server places the bowl of guacamole on the center of the table.

"You're beautiful," he says. "I just love being with you."

I feel happy with Tony, but something rankles, despite this. He says he loves being with me, but not that he loves me. How is it possible that in November he "thought he might be falling in love with me," and yet he still hasn't fallen by January?

"Me too," I say. "Thanks for understanding why I've been spending so much time with my dad right now. I hope you know that you are very special to me. I really care for you a lot."

"I care for you too," he says, squeezing my hand.

Over chicken mole, I update him on my dad's condition.

"You're a really good daughter," he says, patting my arm. "Your dad is really lucky to have you."

Soon, we are sharing ice cream and a second round of margaritas. I have given over to the pleasant feeling of drunkenness, momentarily forgetting about my dad and my family, and just focusing on Tony.

He kisses me on the lips. "You know, Angie, it's been a while since we've spent the night together…a really long while…" He kisses me again.

I pull away slightly. "I just haven't really been in the mood, because of my dad. I'm really sorry."

He puts his hand on my leg. "I understand," he says, "but your dad is going to be okay now, so…do you think you might be in the mood for a sleepover?"

"I'm still staying at my parents," I say, playing with my napkin. "It would be weird if I don't come home, and I'm certainly not bringing you back there."

He moves his hand up my thigh. "Well, what if we just go take a quick detour to your apartment?"

I shake my head. "The keys are at my parents' place."

Tony sighs. "Well, how about we check into a hotel for a few hours?" His hand is now up my skirt.

I pull away. "No, listen. I'm just really tired. That's too much trouble for me right now. Please understand."

He nods. "All right, I'll pay the check, and we'll get you home to your parents," he says.

I get up to go to the restroom. Feeling slightly light headed, I walk into the empty bathroom, go to the sink, and splash water in my face. When I look up in the mirror, I see Tony poking his head into the doorway. I turn around.

"Uh, I think you have the wrong bathroom," I say.

He laughs. "Actually, it kind of looks like we have the place to ourselves. Want to make out a little?"

I shake my head. "What if someone comes in?"

He gestures in the direction of the stall. I giggle. I really wouldn't mind making out a little more. Soon, we are shut inside a stall, kissing like a pair of teenagers.

"What if someone finds us here?" I say between kisses.

"Then I'll pick you up, and they'll only see one pair of legs."

Somehow, in my drunken state, this seems like a plan that would fool anyone, so I continue kissing him. He gropes my breasts, putting his hand down the top of my soft pink sweater. Suddenly, the door swings open, and a pair of high heels click on the tile floor. My heart races, as I realize how truly embarrassing this could be. I do not want to get kicked out of Rosa Mexicano for fooling around in the bathroom. We freeze, and Tony slowly lifts me up. I wrap my legs around his waist. Neither one of us makes a noise as we wait for the woman to apply perfume and lipstick, wash her hands, and then finally leave.

His arms shaking, Tony puts me down.

"That was close," I say, adjusting my shirt and picking up my bag from the ground.

He puts his hands around my waist and kisses me. "Come on," Tony says. "We're alone again." He pushes me back into the wall and kisses my neck, putting his hand up my skirt and pulling down my panties.

"Whoa, Tony, I don't know..."

He unzips his pants. "I want you so bad, Angela. I need you."

"Tony, no. I'm not going to have sex with you in the bathroom of Rosa Mexicano."

His hand still up my skirt, he spreads my legs wider.

"Tony, I'm really serious. Cut it out."

He keeps going, and suddenly, I start to feel scared.

"Get your hands off me. Now!" I say sternly.

Immediately, he takes his hand from under my skirt and backs up.

"God, Angie, I wasn't going to force you."

"I need to go." Hurriedly, I pull up my panties, grab my purse, and run out of the restaurant, leaving him behind in the women's restroom.

Chapter 22

"Afternoon," the doorman said as I ran past him and up the three flights of stairs to our apartment.

"Hi, Mom," I called out as I ran to my bedroom.

I deposited my backpack on my bed, went to the bathroom to wash my face and hands, and then headed to the kitchen to scrounge up an after school snack.

"How was school, Angie?" my mom said.

"Okay." I opened the pantry and began scanning the shelves for something that would tide me over until dinner. "There's nothing to eat," I said.

"I bought those ice cream sandwiches you like," my mom said. "They're in the freezer."

I opened the freezer and took out a Neapolitan-flavored ice cream sandwich.

"Mom," I said, "what was your grandpa's name?"

"Which one?"

"Grandma's dad."

My mom reached into the freezer and took an ice cream sandwich for herself. "His name was Gabriel," she said.

"Gabriel what?"

"Gabriel Thomas."

"I knew it!"

My mom gave me a funny look. "Well of course you did. I've told you before."

"Yeah, but my grandma in my other life told me that his name was George Myers. And you said she was right."

She frowned. "I don't know, honey."

I knew she hated it when I talked about my other life. She always got upset when I did it, even though she tried to hide it. Still, I was really confused. Nothing quite like this had ever happened before. Sure, I had cousins who were different in my different lives. In my alternate reality, my aunts and uncles had had children at different times than they had here. But my great-grandpa? It just wasn't possible.

"But, Mom," I said, "if I have a different great-grandpa in my other life, I wouldn't be the same person. It's not possible."

"Hon, sometimes weird things happen in dreams."

"It's not a dream!" I said.

"Okay, sweetie, whatever you say," my mom said in a voice that let me know that she didn't believe me and that she wouldn't argue with me about it.

I scowled and bolted from the room and into the hallway. I grabbed my sweatshirt from the coatrack and unbolted the lock.

"I'm going to Grandma's!" I shouted as I ran out the door.

I walked the two blocks east slowly, trying to figure out how I was going to solve this mystery. All I knew was that something clearly wasn't adding up. It was already getting cold, and I could see my breath in the air as I walked. I loved the autumn in New York. There was a certain smell in the air, a smell that was absent in California.

"Hi, Bob, I'm here to see my grandma," I said to the doorman of her building.

He knew me well. He had been working there since before I was born, and he had seen me at least once a week since then.

"I'll let her know you're here," he said, pushing a button on the intercom.

I glanced around the lobby. Not much had changed in all the years that I had been coming here. There was still the same slightly stained marble floor, the chandelier, the fake potted plants. And every five years the walls were painted over in the same shade of cream.

"You can go on up," Bob said.

I rode the very cranky elevator to the sixth floor. My grandma was standing in the doorway.

"Come on in," she said. "Grandpa's not here. He went to get his hair cut. You want some cookies?"

"No, thanks," I said, following her into the living room, or the "parlor," as she called it. I sat down on her floral couch and crossed my ankles, waiting for her to sit in the easy chair across from me before I began talking.

"Grandma, something really crazy is going on."

Even though my grandmother did not profess that she believed in my story of alternate universes, she did allow me to talk about them. She once said, "You either have a very active imagination or an incredibly difficult life to handle. Either way, I'm proud of you." I knew that she secretly disagreed with my parents sending me to all these shrinks. She didn't think there was anything wrong with me at all. She was the only one.

"So which is it, Grandma? What was your dad's name?"

"Gabriel Thomas," she said, but as she did, I noticed something very strange. She wasn't looking me in the eye. I had learned all about signs of lying in my junior detective handbook. She was definitely hiding something!

"Come on, Grandma," I said. "What is it that you don't want to tell me?"

"Nothing," she said, her voice clipped. "Let me get you a plate of cookies. You're too skinny. You don't eat enough."

I sighed. "I've never lied to you before. Ever. I wish you wouldn't lie to me."

My grandma stopped and turned around, her face serious. "Angela, I don't want to open a can of worms."

"You won't," I said. "I can keep a secret."

She came and sat beside me on the sofa. "If I tell you something, do you promise never to tell anyone, not even your mother?"

I nodded.

"Well...the man my mother married was Gabriel Thomas. But the man who was actually my father was George Myers."

I looked at her blankly.

"My mother had an affair," she said. "It was with an old boyfriend of hers. My father—that is to say, the man who raised me—he never knew the truth. I didn't even know until my mother was on her deathbed. I wish she hadn't even told me, but I think she just had to get it off her chest, after all those years. I just want to forget I ever found out. My father was my father, as far as I'm concerned. It doesn't matter if it was biological or not."

I nodded, understanding dawning on my face. "So it must be that in my other life, your mom married that guy instead."

"I don't know, sweetie."

"Thanks for telling me, Grandma," I said. "Sorry if I upset you."

"No, it's okay." She squeezed my hand. "I'm glad I don't have to carry that secret alone anymore."

I was home in time for dinner.

Chapter 23

Sunday, January 8, 8:15 p.m., New York

It has now been twelve days since my dad died. I am still very much grieving him. I think it has finally hit me that he really is gone. But I've tried to limit my expression of grief, as much as possible, to my California life. Here, that life seems a world away, especially with my dad right here in the city. I am no longer staying with my parents, as my dad has recovered from his surgery. He still has some chemo treatments, and I will definitely be going to see him whenever he has one, but I have moved back into my own apartment.

If anything good at all came from my father's death, it is that I have grown much closer to my father here and that I cherish every moment we spend together. And my two families have grown closer in ways I never could have imagined. My mother and brother in California seem to have latched on to this idea of my New York family, and as a way of holding on to Dad in some capacity, they have been relaying messages to him, through me. Letting him know how they are doing, telling him a funny joke. It is so surreal for me to have this happen, this merging and blending of my two lives, even in this small way.

In my apartment, I wait for Tony to come and take me out to dinner. The strange episode of last Tuesday hangs heavy over us. We talked on the phone a few times afterward, but neither of us mentioned it. I keep reminding myself that he stopped when I was stern with him. I just didn't like the fact that I had to get stern with him. I feel that he is not very happy about the amount of time I've been spending at my parents' place. But, of course, Tony doesn't know what is really going on. And how do I explain something like that to my boyfriend? *Well, Tony, in an alternate reality, my father actually died of his cancer...*

The buzzer loudly interrupts my thoughts.

"It's me," Tony says.

When I open the door, Tony looks down at me, taking in my knee-high boots and my off-the-shoulder black sweater, and smiles.

"Hi, gorgeous!" He sits on the couch as I search for a pair of earrings in my bedroom.

"I know I've been kind of MIA lately. I didn't want you to think I didn't care about you," I say as I walk back into the living room, putting a silver earring in.

"Oh, trust me. I understand. Your dad had cancer. I get it," he says, grabbing me around the waist and kissing me on the neck.

"I know," I say. "But I'm hoping that now we can spend a lot more time together."

Tony kisses my cheek. "I hope so too. And listen, I feel terrible about the other night. I thought that you were just worried about getting caught. You know that. I was just so drunk, and I really wanted you."

"I know."

"So, are we okay, then?" he says.

I smile. "Yeah, we're okay."

"Hey, I was going to show you over dinner, but I can't wait. I have something for you." He fishes through his brown leather messenger bag and pulls out a copy of the *New Yorker.* He pulls me down to the sofa, flips to the middle of the magazine, and hands it to me.

"I wrote it for you," he says.

In the Silence

If, in the silence, I found my reason
(Knowing of course that reasons are fleeting)
Or if tomorrow my question swims
beneath soapy dishes

Or takes shelter in last week or next month,
Even then,
even then,
the truth pulses in my veins
Waiting for a moment.

"Wow," I say. "No one has ever written me a poem before."

He smiles and squeezes my knee.

"So...what's the truth?" I say.

"The truth...the truth is that I love you."

He loves me. And he chose to tell the world about it, even if only in a way that the two of us would understand.

"I'm actually not all that hungry," he says, nibbling at my ear. "Do you want to stay in?"

"Yeah."

Tony carries me to the bed, somehow managing to remove my skirt and sweater on the way. My boots stay on. My heel makes a hole in my new sheets, and I don't even care. I love this beautiful, wonderful man, and somehow, miraculously, he loves me too.

Friday, February 3, 6:05 p.m., Sacramento

Steve and I are going out to dinner tonight, and I've called a sitter, Maddy, who came highly recommended to me by one of the other moms from Sutterville Preschool. She's sixteen and lives just down the block, near Garcia Bend Park. When the doorbell rings, Ella comes running. She loves to spend time with "big girls." I open the door to reveal a very pretty blond girl wearing a ponytail, jeans, and a tight pink tank top.

"Hi, I'm Maddy," she says. "And you must be Ella!"

"Hi!" Ella replies. "You have big boobies!"

I cringe, but Maddy just laughs and comes inside.

"What do you want to be when you grow up?" Ella says as I hand Maddy the list of important phone numbers.

"I want to be a doctor." Maddy sets a heavy backpack down on the kitchen chair, "And what do you want to be when you grow up?"

Ella grins widely. "I want to be Simba from the *Lion King* and have big boobies just like you!"

I laugh, bite my lip, and turn to Ella. "Why don't you take Maddy up to your room and show her the kitchen set you just got for your birthday?"

I feel bad that Ella's birthday was hardly celebrated this year, coming so soon on the heels of my dad's funeral. I didn't have the energy to throw her a real party, so it was just the three of us. We did, however, give her a very nice kitchen set and a doll that eats, wets itself, and cries when it isn't held enough. Last night, after I remembered why I don't have another baby yet, I took out the doll's batteries and hid them.

Ella grabs Maddy's hand and pulls her upstairs. Steve passes them on the stairs, carrying his shoes.

"That's Maddy, the sitter," I say.

"Nice to meet you, Maddy."

"You too," she yells down, as we walk into the garage.

We have dinner at Fats in Old Sacramento. Walking along the wooden sidewalks of the old wild west–style streets, I hold Steve's hand.

"How are you doing, Angie?" he says, "I know it's been hard."

"Not great," I say, leaning my head on his shoulder. "Thanks for being so supportive. It means a lot to me."

He smiles and squeezes my hand. "I love you," he says.

In the restaurant, I look at Steve sitting across from me, and as much as I love him, I find myself kind of wishing that I was with Tony. When I'm with Tony, everything feels new and exciting and full of passion.

Here, my life is busy and crazy, I'm mourning my dad, and Steve is working a lot. It just isn't a life that's conducive to a lot of passion or romance.

"You thinking about your dad?" Steve says.

I sigh. I have avoided telling Steve about Tony because I didn't want to hurt Steve. But I have never lied to Steve. Ever. And that's one of the things I love about our relationship. I even tell him all about what happens in my other life. In the past, he viewed it as more of an ongoing dream soap opera, fascinated that my dreams could be so detailed and true to life. Now, though, since my dad died, he's stopped referring to my other life as a dream. I'm not sure what he thinks anymore. And that's why it's going to be so hard to tell him about Tony.

"I was thinking about my dad in New York," I say. "He's doing really well, so I'm back in my own apartment now. Kind of back to life as usual. I'm going to be designing a new show, actually, called *Walrus Games,* at Playwright's Horizon…and I'll be spending time with Tony."

"Who's Tony," he says.

"Oh, just this guy I've been seeing there."

"You've been seeing a guy?" He wrinkles his brow.

I swallow. "Um, it's kind of a new relationship," I say, digging into my seafood stir fry.

"I thought you didn't see guys there."

I look down. "It's only been a little over five months."

"Five months isn't really that new of a relationship."

"I know," I say. "I'm kind of…in love with him."

Steve blinks at me. "I always thought it was silly for you to want to remain faithful to me in your dreams. But now, I can't help but wonder what's happened between us that changed that."

"I don't know," I say. "I'm sorry. I'm really sorry."

"God, I don't know what's wrong with me. I have no right to get upset about your dreams. I know I don't. I'm sorry. This is crazy…I know. But I feel like, in some weird way, maybe I did believe in your other life all along. Or maybe I'm just starting to now. After what happened with your dad."

"You're really starting to believe me?" My eyes fill with tears. "I thought you were just like everyone else. I thought you always thought I was crazy. Endearingly crazy. But still crazy."

"Maybe the truth is that we're both crazy. But it's pretty hard to look at the woman you love and respect more than anyone else on earth and think that she's nuts. I just can't do it anymore. I think I'd rather join you on the crazy train."

"Wow. So the Tony thing really upsets you, then? You'd always said it was okay for me to date guys there. You said you didn't care."

"Well, that was when I thought it was nothing but a dream."

I shake my head. "But I believed in it all along, and that didn't matter to you. Besides, I am a different person there. What if I was married there too? Would you expect me to get a divorce?"

He wipes his mouth on his napkin. "You aren't married there, so that's not an issue. You *are* married to me."

"But what if it *is* just a dream?" I say.

"You can't have it both ways, Angie."

The piece of bread catches in my throat. How can Steve think he has the right to dictate what I do in a life he isn't even sure he believes in? Even so, I have a small, nagging feeling of guilt. I was the one who always insisted that I shouldn't sleep with anyone there after I married Steve. Why did I suddenly feel so differently?

Saturday, February 4, 10:20 p.m., New York

I spent all day yesterday and today thinking about the conversation I had with Steve, and I'm still no closer to finding a real solution. I understand why Steve feels the way he does. But I feel like it's too late. I love Tony too much to give him up now.

And how could I explain this to Tony? *I'm dumping you because my alternate reality husband doesn't want me to cheat on him.*

But more importantly, I don't want to break up with him. He makes me feel beautiful. He loves me. He's great in bed. And, naively perhaps, growing up I had always assumed I'd eventually get married and be happy in both lives. I never expected to fall so deeply in love with Steve that it was hard for me to be with anyone else. But now I feel like things are falling into place. I should be allowed to be happy in both of my lives. It will hurt me tremendously to lie to Steve, but I see no other way. Any other choice will deeply hurt a man I love.

Chapter 24

Sunday, February 5, 3:30 p.m., Sacramento

Ella and I are at Fairytale Town in Land Park, a play area based on fairy tales and nursery rhymes. Ella loves to run around the pirate ship from *Peter Pan* and slide down the rabbit hole from *Alice in Wonderland.*

"Mommy, I'm gonna run around the crooked mile!" Ella says.

"Okay, El," I say. "You can run the mile, but just one loop around, and then come right back, okay?"

"Okay!" she says, taking off with the other kids. I decide to get a drink from a drinking fountain while Ella is running around. As I turn the corner, the world starts to fade and bleed like a watercolor. *No. Please, no.*

Sunday, February 5, 6:33 a.m., New York

"Angie, wake up." Tony is shaking me.

"What is it?" I say, rubbing my eyes.

He looks pale and clammy. "I think I'm sick. Do you have any Pepto-Bismol or anything like that?"

"Yeah, Tony, I think there is some in the medicine cabinet. Didn't you check there?"

He shakes his head. "I wanted to ask first."

"Well, you don't have to ask. Just use it. Maybe you should go sleep on the couch." I try to quell the panic rising in my chest. Ella isn't going to know where I am. What if someone takes her? "Please, Tony, doctor's orders are for a full twelve hours, remember?"

"Yeah, but I'm sick. It's not such a big deal, is it?"

I try to remain calm. "No, just make sure I don't wake up again, all right?"

"Okay," he says, walking out of the room. I close my eyes tightly, trying desperately to fall asleep, but feeling pretty wide awake. *Please.* And then, the world gives way.

Sunday, February 5, 3:38 p.m., Sacramento

"Ma'am, ma'am, are you okay?" A strange man is propping me up into a sitting position.

I open my eyes. "My daughter, where's my daughter?"

"I'm not sure," he says. "I think you just passed out."

I shake my head. "No, I'm um…I'm a narcoleptic. I just fell asleep, but I'm fine now. I just need to find my daughter. She was at the crooked mile."

The man helps me to my feet, and I take off running. "Thanks!" I yell behind me as I round the corner, my mind running through the possibilities of what could have happened. But there, sitting calmly on a bench, is Ella.

I run to her and hug her. "Oh, thank God you're all right."

"Where did you go, Mommy?"

"I'm sorry, baby. Mommy fell asleep. But you were very good to wait here for me. That was the right thing to do. And if that ever happens again, ask another mommy or one of the workers to help you, okay?"

She looks up at me with huge brown eyes. "I was scared."

"I know," I say, squeezing her hand. "Let's go catch the bus home. I think we've had enough Fairytale Town today."

She nods.

Sunday, February 5, 12:00 p.m., New York

I open the door of my bedroom to find Tony sitting on the couch, reading the *Times*. He has significantly more color to him now.

"How are you feeling?" I say.

"A lot better after I threw up," he says. "This is so embarrassing. I really hope you don't catch this."

"Do you want me to make you something to eat? Toast and tea maybe?"

He smiles. "Toast would be nice. You aren't mad I woke you up, are you?"

I open the refrigerator and take out the whole wheat bread. "I'm not mad." I pop the bread into the toaster and put some water in my old, cracked teakettle.

"Tony," I say, "have you ever heard or read anything about alternate realities? Do you think they might exist?"

He looks askance at me. "Oh yeah, my sister is all into that shit. Magical crystals, energy fields, alternate realities, psychics, past lives. The money she has blown seeing fortune-tellers...It's enough to drive the whole family nuts. Especially my parents because they're Greek Orthodox. She's kind of batty. I love my sister, but I have pity on her husband. I could never put up with that."

I feel like I've just been hit with a ton of bricks. I guess for now I'll have to stick with the narcolepsy story.

"Why do you ask?" he says. The kettle whistles, and I pour his hot water in a cup and add a tea bag.

"Oh, I don't know," I say. "It's just that whenever I sleep, I continue the same dream exactly where I left off, where I'm married and I have a daughter and live in California. My parents think it might be an alternate reality." I laugh nervously.

"That's cool. Sounds like a very involved dream." He smiles at me. "You're so imaginative. It's cute."

"I don't have any milk or sugar. Sorry."

"I'll just drink it black."

"Anyway," I say, "I do want to explain my condition to you better. See, because you woke me up last night, it disturbed my REM sleep cycle. So now today, I'll probably fall asleep a few times uncontrollably, and even if I don't, I'm just going to feel really tired and shitty all day. I know it seems silly that I can't be woken up and that I have to get up so late. I'm not easy to live with. I'm not going to lie. But it really is important that I get those full uninterrupted twelve hours of sleep. Okay?"

"Sure," he says, munching his toast. "Yeah, no problem."

Chapter 25

EIGHTH GRADE WAS no fun at all. In elementary school, there was a colorfully decorated classroom where we sat at "table groups" and had class parties for holidays, complete with copious amounts of sugar. A typical science activity was building a mountain from paper-mâché. In just two short years, however, school had transformed into a sort of florescent-lit prison with desks. Now we had to sit alone (no talking), and science consisted of writing research papers. Holidays were just ordinary days, and there were so many teachers that it was hard to get to know them. Worst of all, the amount of homework had increased, so instead of coming home from school, doing a little homework, and playing or watching television, I now came home from an eight-hour school day to face four more hours of homework. We had all the work of high school with none of the fun: there were no football games, no prom, and no cute high school boys. Eighth grade was no fun at all.

My school in California was a typical middle school. We walked from building to building outside. Because the school had grown overcrowded in the last couple of years, several of my classes were held in portable buildings, quite far away from the rest of the campus.

One day in February, I walked quickly from the gym to the math building at the front of the school, avoiding the muddy grass. I had to hurry, or I was going to be late for my algebra test. About ten yards from the building, the bell rang. I exhaled sharply and ran the rest of the way.

When I entered the classroom, the other students were all seated at their desks.

"You're late, Angela," Mr. Loehman said. "That's five minutes in detention."

I felt my cheeks grow hot. After the two hours of algebra homework I did last night, I was really not in the mood for this.

"That's not fair," I said, trying to stay calm. "I had PE, and I only had five minutes to change my clothes and get across campus. Plus I had to use the restroom, and there was a line."

"Sorry," he said. "You should have waited to use the restroom until after your next class."

"I couldn't wait! I had to go then. There's no way I could take a test when I had to go to the bathroom."

I heard other students snickering.

"Sorry, Angela, not my problem," he said.

He was such a jerk. I could feel tears building behind my eyes. Why did I always cry when I was angry? It was so embarrassing.

"Come on, Mr. Loehman," said John, one of the cool skater guys. "Give the girl a break. She had to pee!"

Now I could see that Mr. Loehman was getting flustered. And that wasn't good for anyone.

"Take your seat. You will have five minutes of detention. No more arguing."

John looked like he was about to say something else

"Or the whole class will have detention."

At that, the room went silent. Mr. Loehman began handing out the tests. I wanted to cry so badly, but I just wasn't going to give him that satisfaction. I bit my lip.

When he tossed my test onto my desk, I glared at him, but he looked away. I opened the test and began working on the first problem, trying to remember all of the algorithms I had studied the night before. So far, the test was easy. I clicked away at my calculator and then scrawled my answer in pencil. I continued, working up through question ten, confident that I was getting every problem correct. And then I read the directions for questions ten to twenty. All ten questions had to do with graphing radical functions! My vision blurred with unshed tears. I hated Mr. Loehman. We hadn't learned how to graph radical functions, at least not officially. There was an extra-credit question on the homework last night that dealt with radical functions, but it was *extra credit.* That meant you didn't have to do it. And I hadn't. Of course, I also hadn't read the entire chapter like I was supposed to, and now I had no idea how to do the last ten questions on the text. But if I left them blank, even if I got all the other questions correct, I would only get a score of 50 percent...a failing score. I was so angry that my hands were shaking. But I knew talking to Mr. Loehman about it would do no good. He was already angry at me for being late and arguing with him.

Normally, I didn't cheat in school. But I felt like Mr. Loehman had cheated by giving us this unfair test. I snuck a glance at Amber, who was sitting on my right, but she was covering her paper with her arm. Out of the corner of my eye, I looked at Brett, to my left. He looked as confused as I was. So...there was no hope of copying off of anyone else.

And then I had an idea. If I could just go into my other life right now, I could look it up in my Algebra textbook there. Then I could come back here and finish the test. Of course, there were a few problems with this plan. For one thing, it depended on my being able to fall asleep. But after staying up so late last night, I *was* pretty tired. It also depended on my being able to teach myself fast and get back here in time to finish the test. Still, even if I didn't have time to finish all the problems, at least I might be able to get a passing score. And it was the only idea I had.

Furtively, I leaned forward on my desk, putting my head on my fist as though concentrating deeply. I let my hair fall over my eyes. *Fall asleep.* I breathed slowly, letting myself relax fully, and listened to the rhythmic ticking of the clock and the scratching of pencils.

And then I woke up in my bed in New York. I felt groggy, and it took a moment for me to remember what was happening. I rubbed my eyes. But then it all came back to me. I bolted from the bed and grabbed my algebra book from my desk, frantically flipping through the table of contents. *Radical functions, radical functions...*And then I saw it. Chapter 7.8: "Graphing Radical Functions." I opened the book to that page and began to read. It was confusing, but I forced myself to focus. I read and reread the instructions. Then I attempted the practice problem. I flipped to the back of the book to the answer section. Practice question 7.8...I did it right! I glanced at my digital alarm clock. Good, I had only been awake for ten minutes. There was still time to finish the test. I stood up...and the world went black.

Someone was shaking my arm.

"Angela, you fell asleep," Mr. Loehman said, shaking his head.

"Sorry." I picked up my pencil. "I'm narcoleptic, remember?"

Mr. Loehman walked back to his desk. *Remember.* I looked at question ten again and then at the clock. I still had ten minutes. I could do this.

Furiously, I made my way through the final ten problems. Just as I finished the last one, the bell rang.

"Pencils down," Mr. Loehman said.

I laughed. I had actually gotten away with it.

The next morning in New York, my mother found me asleep on the floor, my algebra textbook beside me. "I think someone's been studying too hard," she said.

A week later, we got our test results back. On the top of my paper, in red felt-tip marker, it read 100 percent. I did it!

"Angela, would you please see me after class?" Mr. Loehman said.

I gulped. Did he know I cheated? But no, there was no way he could possibly know. "Sure," I said.

After class, I walked up to Mr. Loehman' desk.

"Angela," he said, "I'm sorry about giving you that detention the other day. I just get really frustrated with everyone being late so much and always having excuses about it. But you are the only one in the class who got those graphing questions right. I can see that you've really been putting a lot of work into this class. So anyway, don't worry about the detention. You don't have to serve it. And keep up the good work, okay?"

He smiled at me, and I felt absolutely overwhelmed with guilt. "Okay, thanks," I said, wishing I could sink through the floor.

My cheeks burned as I walked home. When I got there, I ran straight upstairs and tore my test into hundreds of pieces before burying it at the bottom of my trash can. The last thing I needed was for my parents to make a big deal about my perfect score.

When I returned downstairs, my mom asked me if I had gotten my test back.

"Yep," I said. "But I don't want to talk about it."

"That bad?" Jonathan said, looking up from behind *The Catcher in the Rye.*

I was nearly silent as I ate my burrito at dinner. I felt terrible that Mr. Loehman thought I was some kind of a math genius now and especially that he thought I really cared about his class. I still didn't like him that much, but now I just felt kind of sorry for him. I sighed. There was nothing I could do now. There was no way to explain how I had cheated. I would just have to forget about it. But I wouldn't do it again, I decided. That was…unless I really needed to.

Chapter 26

Wednesday, February 14, 5:31 p.m., Sacramento

It is Valentine's Day today, and Steve came home from work with a bouquet of yellow roses, my favorite. He kisses me. Ella is spending the night with her grandma tonight, which means the pressure is on for romance tonight.

I've cooked some roast pork loin, asparagus, and wild rice, which we eat by candlelight.

"Pork's a little tough," Steve says.

"Sorry," I say, a shade of annoyance in my voice.

"That's okay. Thanks for cooking." He turns his attention back to his plate.

After our earlier conversation, I lied to Steve for the first time in our marriage and told him that I broke up with Tony. Can he tell? And can he tell how angry I am that for all these years he insisted my other life was nothing but a dream and that now, when he finally begins to believe me, he tries to dictate what I can do there? I try to squash down my feelings. Tonight is supposed to be special.

After dinner, I follow Steve upstairs.

I lie down on the bed, and Steve starts to kiss me, but I can't help wishing I were with Tony instead, who isn't angry at me. As if by rote, Steve gropes at my breasts. I lie there and look up at the ceiling. I wonder whether it might be time to paint the room. Maybe cream would be nice?

"Are you okay, honey? What's wrong?" Steve says, looking searchingly at me.

"Nothing," I say. "I'm fine."

I close my eyes, stopping my brain from thinking. It helps. Without making a conscious decision, I begin to imagine that it is Tony kissing me, instead of Steve. "Tony," I say. And then my eyes fly open. I realize what I've said as soon as the word crosses my lips. The look on Steve's face makes me want to cry. He gets up and begins getting dressed.

I feel terrible.

Silently, Steve walks out of the room and goes downstairs.

Thursday, March 2, 6:09 p.m., Sacramento

I stir my tomato sauce, while Ella stands next to me on her step stool.

"Okay, you be the taste tester, Ella. What does it need?" I say, holding out the wooden spoon so she can lick it.

She thinks for a moment. "More pepper!"

"You sure you want it spicy?"

"Me and Daddy like it spicy."

I wipe some sauce off of her upper lip with my finger, when the phone rings.

"Hello?"

"Hi, Angie." It's Steve.

"Hey, where are you? You coming home soon?"

"Um, actually, I have a lot of work to get done here. I have to meet with these people tomorrow, and I really need to get the CAD file spiffed up a little bit before the meeting. I'll probably be home sometime after eleven."

"Eleven?" I say. "Steve, your daughter misses you. You've come home after she's asleep every night this week."

"I know," he says. "Tell her I love her and I'll play baseball with her this weekend, okay?"

"Fine," I say, and I hang up.

Since Valentine's Day, things have gone from bad to worse. We haven't even attempted sex since that night. I don't feel in the mood to pretend I'm in the mood. He's responded by retreating into his work. And that makes me furious. It's one thing to neglect me, but it's another to not be here for his daughter.

Ella looks at me with a pout. "I want Daddy!" she says.

I sigh. I want my daddy too. I want to ask him what I should do to fix things with Steve. I want to ask him whether I should stay with Tony. But my dad isn't here. And my New York dad doesn't even know Steve. I slam the lid down on the pot. Why did my dad have to die? I need him, and he isn't here.

Ella looks at me with tears in her eyes.

"I know you want your daddy, baby, but Daddy has to work so he can earn money to take care of us." The last thing I want is for Ella to think her dad is upset with her. "And he wants to play baseball with you on Saturday, okay?"

She considers this. "Okay, but I want to do the batting every single time."

I pick her up and set her down on the floor. "Sure, honey."

Wednesday, March 8, 12:30 p.m., Sacramento

Today is my day to work at Sutterville Preschool. I am in charge of the craft station. I give each kid a cardboard shoe box with a piece of paper and three marbles inside. The kids squirt whatever colors of paint they want into the box and roll the marbles around, creating a marbled painting effect on the paper. Despite the newspaper spread over the floor, the kids are making quite a mess.

Ella, usually independent, has been by my side since we got here. She has already done the project three times.

"Ella, are you sure you don't want to play outside or read a book or something?" I say.

"No," she says, hugging my legs. "I want to be by you."

"Okay. Why don't you help the other kids do their projects?"

And she doesn't leave my side the rest of the day. We leave with five marbled paintings. I let her choose her favorite to put up on the fridge.

"There, that looks great."

"I wanna show Daddy," she says.

True to his word, Steve did spend time with Ella last weekend. He played baseball with her and took her to the movies. He didn't invite me. We are hardly even speaking at this point. I think it's clear that he knows I'm lying, but I don't know what to say, because he's right. I know that, more than anything, he's hurt that I'm more interested in Tony than I am in him. Even if Tony might not really exist.

This morning, Steve told me that he is going to spend the weekend at his parents' house in Vacaville because it's his dad's birthday. He didn't ask me to come, even though he never goes away without me. I didn't respond. To ask to come would mean to face questions about Tony, which I couldn't answer truthfully. He left for work, and I haven't been able to think about anything else since.

I call my mom.

"Hey, Mom, do you want to come over and have a little tea party? I need to talk."

"Well, sure, honey," she says. "Just let me get a load of laundry in, and I'll be right over."

It's times like this that I'm really glad my mom lives only a few blocks away. I put a pot of tea on and then wash my face. By the time I finish, I hear my mom's car pull up in the driveway.

When my mom comes inside, she can tell something is wrong right away. Wasting no time, she sets Ella up with some YouTube videos.

We sit down at the table, and I pour the tea.

"Okay, Angie, what's going on?" she says.

"Steve and I are having problems, Mom. Bad problems."

She looks concerned. "I thought you and Steve had a great marriage. What's the problem?"

"Well…" I sigh. "I told Steve about this guy I've been seeing in my other life in New York. Tony. And I guess I've just been really preoccupied with Tony. To the exclusion of Steve. He's been working all the time." I lower my voice. "He told me that I had to break up with Tony."

My mom takes a sip of her tea. "So did you?"

"No."

"Why not?"

"Because it isn't like we just started dating. It's been six months. And I'm in love with him. And I don't want to hurt Tony."

"But you don't mind hurting Steve?" my mom says pointedly.

"Yes, Mom, I do mind hurting Steve, actually. I'm consumed with guilt. But it isn't like I'm really cheating on him. For all we know, that life could be nothing but a dream."

My mom shakes her head. "Mmm, no, Angie, come on. It's still emotionally cheating, if nothing else. Steve is your husband. You've been with him for twelve years. You had his child. And you want to throw that away so that you can knock boots with some guy in New York?"

"Knock boots? Where did you even hear that term, Mom?"

"HBO. I've been watching a lot of TV since your father died. Anyway, don't try to change the subject. It's very convenient that now you try to claim your New York life is a dream. But I know you don't believe that. Besides, that would mean that your dad...he'd really be gone then."

I feel like I've been punched in the stomach. I completely expected my mom to back me up, to tell me that Steve was being a selfish jerk.

"I can't believe you agree with him! Dad would have understood," I say. Then I start to cry. "Mom, I miss Daddy. I miss him."

My mom's eyes tear up. "I know, honey. I miss him too." She hugs me, and we cry together.

"I'm not trying to make you feel bad, Angie. I just don't want to see you lose Steve."

I shrug. "I won't lose him. He would never leave me now that we have Ella."

"There is more than one way to lose someone," my mom says quietly.

"What do I do, Mom?" I whisper.

"You stop dating this other guy. You stop thinking about this other guy. And you work on your marriage."

I stand up. "You just don't understand. It isn't that easy. It's really serious with Tony. I can't just end it. I can't."

"Look, Angie," my mom says. "You asked what I think you should do, and that's what I think. You aren't going to listen to me if you don't want to. So do things your way. Maybe Steve will accept the situation in time. I don't know. We'll see."

"Well," I say as I put our teacups in the sink, "do you have any advice on how I might be able to help him accept it?"

My mom thinks for a moment. "I think that regardless of whether or not you break things off with Tony, you and Steve and Ella need to reconnect as a family. Maybe you should take a family vacation."

I smile. My mom is right. If I can just get Steve to see that I still love him, that he's important to me, then maybe he will be able to forgive me.

Chapter 27

Saturday, March 11, 7:15 p.m., New York

I AM WAITING outside the movie theater at Union Square for Tony to meet me. I clutch my red suede coat tighter around me as the wind blows my ponytail around. It is a clear, beautiful night, but cold. I glance at my watch. Meeting Tony makes me feel like a kid ditching class. But in this case, there isn't much chance I'll get caught. I tap my boots on the cement. One thing I do know, though, is that I am not going to do this to Steve just for a fling.

I feel someone grab me around the waist and hug me from behind. It's Tony. I turn around, and he kisses me.

"I bought the tickets," I say.

Tony flicks my ponytail with his hand.

"Okay, then let's go."

As we take three sets of escalators, Tony keeps one hand clutched around my waist, the other on the hip of my jeans as he stands behind me, one step down.

We head into the theater and sit in the back, up at the top, so that we have the best view.

"We don't need this," I say, smiling, lifting up the arm that is between our plush movie theater chairs.

Tony draws me into his arms.

After the movie, we go across the street to Cosi and make s'mores at the table, roasting the marshmallows over the little flame.

I have so much fun with Tony. The thought of ending things between us is too painful to even contemplate.

I take a gooey marshmallow off the metal skewer and sandwich it, with a piece of chocolate, between two graham crackers.

"Tony, do you think we have a future together?" I say.

Tony coughs.

"Are you okay?"

"Yeah," he says, wiping coffee off his chin.

"Sorry. I didn't mean to throw that at you like that."

"That's okay. You just caught me a little by surprise...Well, we've been dating, what, six months or so now? I love you. You love me. All good signs, right?"

I take a bite of my s'more and then a sip of coffee. "Yeah, good signs. But... are you thinking long term with me?"

"Well, wherever it leads, Angie. If things are good, I see no reason to break up."

I smile. "Good. Because I'm thinking long term, Tony. I'm just going to say that right now. I'm not in any rush to get married or anything like that. But I'm not looking to waste my time."

He nods. "I don't want to waste your time either. I just think we need to sit back and let this go wherever it's going to go. You know I love you, right?"

"Right." I say, smiling. I'm already married with a kid in one life. It doesn't need to happen immediately here.

When I get home, I notice a text from Jana.

"Hey, Angie, how you doing? Call me. I miss you. Bye."

I sigh. I really have neglected my friends lately. I'll call her tomorrow, I think, heading into my bedroom.

Sunday, March 12, 8:08 p.m., Sacramento

The weekend has been difficult without Steve. Ella misses him a lot, I feel resentful that he left, and my bed is very empty without him.

I hear the garage door open. I put my book down and sigh. He's home late. Poor Ella is already asleep. We can't go on like this. I meet Steve at the door to the garage, in one of his old Kings T-shirts. I've been sleeping in it all weekend, and my small frame swims in the huge shirt.

"Hey, you," I say. "Are you still my friend?"

Steve walks to the kitchen counter and puts his keys down. "I don't know, Ang. Are you my friend?"

I nod my head.

"Where's Ella?"

"She's in bed, Steve, where do you think? I know you hate me right now, but that does not give you an excuse to abandon your daughter. She needs you. Her grandpa died, and now you aren't here for her. Some father you are." I regret the words as soon as I say them.

Steve's eyes fill with tears. "I love Ella more than anything. You know that."

I close my eyes. "I'm sorry. I know you do. Just, please, I'm begging you—don't do this to her. She really needs you."

"I know...I'll call in sick tomorrow, okay?"

"Okay," I say.

Lying in bed next to Steve, I feel lonelier than when he wasn't here at all. He is scrunched on the end of the bed as far from me as humanly possible. I miss him. I reach out my hand and touch his shoulder.

"Please, Steve," I whisper.

"I'm sorry, Angie. I just can't right now. I know you'll only be thinking of him."

I turn onto my stomach and gaze out the window. The street is wet from rain, and it reflects the glow of the streetlights. It looks like a setting for a film noir. Steve loves film noir. When we were first dating, we sat in his dorm room and worked our way through almost all of them: *Double Indemnity*, *The Blue Angel*, *The Maltese Falcon*, *Chinatown*. I miss those days. I turn back onto my side and close my eyes, blinking back tears.

Chapter 28

I WAS CURLED up with Steve on his twin mattress, on the top of a bunk bed he shared with his roommate, Scott. The mattress was cheap, stuffed with foam, and covered in a waterproof casing designed to make it last through as many college students as possible. It was one of the less desirable aspects of dorm life—we had to share a bed barely big enough for one. I always made Steve sleep on the outside. There was no safety bar, and I had visions of tumbling to my death in the middle of the night. Still, it was cozy. And definitely preferable to being in my own room with my horror of a roommate, a girl who had actually posted a list of "Roommate Rules" on the wall, including such gems as "Mugs are to be put in the cupboard handle side out" and "Written permission shall be requested for overnight guests."

Steve drew me closer, and I snuggled against his chest, relishing in the warmth of his body. And then we heard it yet again: the shrieking, piercing whine, so loud we had to cover our ears. It was the third time this week, but the first to occur so late at night. Ah yes, the favorite pastime of drunken freshmen: pulling the fire alarm. Steve and I both sat up and climbed down the side of the bed. I was wearing my favorite pajamas, pink linen shorts and a T-shirt with a picture of a frog, which read "Your pad or mine?" I grabbed a sweatshirt and slid my feet into a pair of flip-flops before we headed outside into the cold for the long wait until we would be let back into the building.

Outside, I leaned against Steve, shivering slightly. It was December and only forty degrees, which was very cold for California.

"Your little nose is turning pink," he said, kissing the tip of it.

"Yeah, well, I'm not exactly dressed for the weather," I said, gesturing to my bare legs, now covered in goose bumps.

"It's okay. You look sexy this way."

"What way? Freezing?"

"No," he said, laughing, "half naked."

I shook my head, grinning. Since Steve and I had first slept together, a month ago, he could hardly think about anything else, it seemed.

"Okay," I said, "get your mind out of the gutter. I'm beginning to think that's all you think I'm good for."

Steve pinched my butt. "You made me wait a year. You know I love you for you."

I smiled, knowing it was true. Steve hadn't pressured me, even though I knew he was desperate to lose his virginity, which had become a sort of liability to him at age nineteen. He waited until I was truly ready, and when we finally did have sex, I remembered with a sort of shock that I was a virgin too, at least in this life. I bled a little, but nothing compared to what happened with Dan. Steve was understanding and patient; he took his time. And I had never regretted being with him for a moment.

Steve rubbed his hands up and down my arms, trying to warm me up.

"Poor baby, you're really cold," he said. "I thought you were used to all that New York cold." He winked at me.

I smacked his arm playfully. "You said you didn't believe in alternate realities."

"I don't, really. But I do think it's pretty entertaining. I mean, who has the same continuous dream every night? It's awesome. It's like your own little TV series."

"Or my *life*," I said.

"Right. Or your life. We'll never know which."

Finally, the firefighters showed up, confirmed there was no actual fire, and allowed us back into the building. We filed up the stairs amid the throngs of other sleepy students.

Steve unlocked the door to his room, and we stepped inside, shedding our sweatshirts. The heat was up so high that I could already feel myself beginning to sweat. I opened the window a crack, letting a gust of cold air in.

"I'm glad Scott went home for the weekend," Steve said, putting his arms around me.

"Me too. It's nice to be alone together. Even if we do have to sleep in a tiny bed." I giggled.

"I promise you, Angie, once we get married, I'll buy you the biggest bed they make."

I swallowed. Married? Did I hear him right?

"Um, how do you know we'll end up getting married?" I said.

Steve hugged me tighter. "Of course we'll get married, love bug. Once we graduate college."

I laughed. "Wow, you've got it all figured out, don't you? Did it ever occur to you to ask *my* opinion?"

Steve pulled away and looked down into my eyes. I tried to look serious, but I couldn't hide the twinkle in my eye. Of course I wanted to marry Steve! Still, I didn't want him to just think he could plan out our whole future without even consulting me.

"Sorry," Steve said. "I did sort of get ahead of myself. Let me try this again."

And suddenly he was down on one knee, holding my hand. "Angela, I love you more than anyone else in the world, and I want to spend the rest of my life with you and grow old with you. Will you marry me?"

I couldn't help but compare this to the "proposal" I received from Dan in my New York world, really nothing more than a thinly veiled lie to get me into bed. No, this was heartfelt. This was real. But at the same time, I couldn't quite believe it was actually happening.

"Really?" I said. "Do you mean it for real?"

"Of course."

"Then yes!" I said. "Yes!" And I got down beside him on the floor and threw myself into his arms.

We kissed and kissed, giddy with excitement. When we finally came up for air, we realized that we had rolled all the way across the room. I laughed, crawling into his lap.

Steve took my hand. "I'm sorry I don't have a ring for you. I wasn't really planning to propose tonight. But don't worry. I'm going to save up my money, and I'll buy you a beautiful diamond ring soon. Or at least...before the wedding."

"It's okay," I said. "I don't care about the ring. All that matters is that we're engaged." I jumped up. "I have to call my mom!"

"Whoa," Steve said. "It's the middle of the night, Angie. Why don't you call her tomorrow? Tonight it will be our special secret."

"Okay," I said.

Most of my friends thought I was crazy, getting engaged before I was even out of college. They asked me how I could possibly know that Steve was the *one*. But all I could say was, I just *knew*. I felt like I'd been waiting my whole life to meet him. And when I did, it was as if I'd met the other half of myself.

Chapter 29

Monday, March 13, 2:42 p.m., Sacramento

I KEPT ELLA home from Sutterville today so that she could spend time with her dad. The two of them went on a bike ride and played soccer. Now, they are sitting at the table, eating grilled cheese sandwiches.

I mix a glass of chocolate milk for Ella, frothing it in the blender with cocoa and sugar, the way she likes it.

"Steve?" I say. "I was thinking that it would be really nice if we all went to Lake Tahoe this weekend. It's been in the eighties all week, so it should be nice." I hand Ella her chocolate milk.

She snaps to attention. "Lake Tahoe? Yay! Let's go!"

"I don't know, honey," he says. "I have a lot of work I need to get done."

"But wouldn't this be the perfect opportunity for you to spend some quality time with your daughter?"

Ella looks at him expectantly. "You're right. Maybe just you and me can go, how would that be, El? We can spend some time together."

Her lip pouts out. "No," she says, beginning to tear up, "I want Mommy *and* Daddy!"

I look at Steve triumphantly. "Okay, Ella, okay. Don't cry," he says. "We'll all go."

After they finish eating, Ella goes into the backyard to play on the swing set Steve built for her. Steve brings the plates to the kitchen.

"Steve, please, won't you talk to me? We need to talk. I'll get a babysitter, and we can go to Caffé Latte."

He sighs. "All right. We'll talk."

Steve goes to watch TV, and I call Maddy. I tell her it's okay to bring her homework with her and that we'll be home early.

I take my hair out of its ponytail and shake my head around, then quickly change into a deep crimson shirt. Steve's favorite.

"Oh, Mama, you look chic," Ella says.

"Really? *Chic*? Where did you learn that word?"

"Chic and fableous."

I laugh. "That's fab*u*lous, sweetheart. And thanks."

At six o'clock, Maddy comes over, to Ella's great delight, and Steve and I drive to the shopping center on Pocket Road. We don't really talk on the way. Soon, we are sitting at a picnic table outside of Caffé Latte, drinking Mexican mochas.

"So? You said you wanted to talk."

I take a sip of my coffee. "Steve, do you still love me?"

Steve looks sad. "I'll love you forever, Angie."

I want to cry. "I love you too," I say. "Nothing can change that. I need you to know that. I need you to understand that, here, you are the only one I ever have loved."

"That's all you can give me?" he says.

I look down and don't answer.

Wednesday, March 15, 1:20 p.m., New York

Jana and I are walking up Sixth Avenue after having had Frappuccinos at Starbucks.

"Are you hungry?" I say.

"Yeah, I'm starving. Do you want to get lunch somewhere?"

"Sure, but don't you need to get back to work?"

"I never take long lunches. No one will even notice." Then she looks up. "Ooh, let's eat at Olive Garden."

I groan. "I worked there all through college, remember? I don't think I could stomach it."

"Come on," she says. "I want unlimited soup and salad."

"I used to hate having to bring out all that soup and salad. It's more work than normal, and you get practically no tip for it."

Jana grabs my arm. "We'll leave a big tip. Let's go."

Inside, the hostess seats us in a big booth overlooking Sixth Avenue. I don't recognize anyone working here; it's been too long. But I do recognize many of the items on the menu. I end up ordering whole wheat pasta with Alfredo sauce.

"So," Jana says, "how's life?"

"Well, Tony wrote me a poem and told me he loves me."

"How's the sex?"

I blush.

"That good, huh?" She laughs. "So when's the wedding?"

"I don't know," I say, taking a sip of raspberry lemonade.

"But there will be one in the future, huh?"

"Maybe," I say. "We're going to take our time, just see where the relationship leads."

She nods. "So he's afraid to commit, then?"

"No." I glare at her. "We just don't want to rush things."

"Okay, as long as you're happy. Do you have a key to his place yet?"

I shake my head, taking a bite of a breadstick. "Not yet. But we sleep at each other's places all the time, so I think things are heading in that direction."

She smiles. "Well, good. And you know where to send the wedding invitation when the time comes."

Friday, March 17, 4:55 p.m., Lake Tahoe

"When are we gonna get there?" Ella says, kicking her legs against her seat.

Steve's jaw flexes. "Ten minutes after you stop asking."

"Really, soon, Ella," I say. "Try to be a patient little girl now."

"I'm not a little girl!" Ella says. "I'm four. I'm a big girl now."

"Well, big girls don't whine. Big girls sit quietly in their seats until they arrive at Lake Tahoe."

Ella's mouth snaps shut, and she looks out the window.

I remember last year when we drove up here, we were talking and laughing all the way. We sang songs with Ella and played I Spy. Now, the car is silent. As we drive higher into the mountains, I feel more peaceful. I love the big pine trees lining the hills, and shading the road, and knowing that, in the distance, beautiful Lake Tahoe glimmers in the sunlight.

By the time we arrive at the cabin, Ella is fast asleep in her car seat. I unstrap her, pick her up, and look up at the cute little two-bedroom cottage. Steve begins unloading our suitcases from the car, while I bring in the bag of groceries.

As I sauté the artichoke hearts, olives, tomatoes, and garlic, Steve blends fresh basil, parmesan cheese, olive oil, and pine nuts to make the pesto sauce. Ella sits on the plaid flannel couch and watches *The Price is Right* on a television that has a slightly green tint to it. We are the picture of the perfect family. We used to actually be a perfect family.

Chapter 30

Saturday, March 18, 1:22 p.m., Lake Tahoe

THIS MORNING, WE got up and ate cereal, and I packed us a picnic lunch of pita bread and hummus, deviled eggs, and fruit with brie. Then the three of us walked to the beach, Ella on Steve's shoulders, me carrying a blow-up rowboat.

At the lake, I lie on a towel on the warm sand, letting the sun heat my body and relax me. Steve sits next to me, reading a book, while Ella builds a sand castle.

"Can we go swimming, Daddy?" Ella says, poking her dad in the arm.

He puts down his book. "Okay, little girl."

Ella looks offended.

"I mean, okay *big* girl," Steve says. Then he takes out her water wings and puts one on her left arm.

"No," she says, "I'm a big girl now."

"Big girls wear water wings until big girls learn to swim," he says, putting the other orange inflated device on her right arm.

I watch as Steve and Ella run down to the water, Steve in his blue board shorts, Ella in her little pink polka-dotted one-piece. Because it's a lake, there aren't really waves, which is a good thing for Ella. They begin to wade in, and Ella shrieks as she puts her feet in the cold water. Steve picks her up and walks in up to his waist.

I close my eyes. My eyelids look orange from the inside, with the sun beating down on my face. I open the bottle of sunscreen and spread some more on my cheeks and nose and then on my body, around my white bikini.

Steve is trying to teach Ella to paddle in the water, and she is swimming around with her water wings on. I lie back down and turn over onto my stomach, feeling at peace and almost happy. Almost.

About fifteen minutes later, Steve and Ella come back, dripping and laughing. I hand Ella her Barbie beach towel and help her remove her water wings. She cuddles up to me, sitting on my lap, her wet hair tickling my chin.

"Mommy, take me on the boat."

I glance at Steve. "Maybe Daddy wants to take you."

"I think Mommy will take you." Steve picks up his book.

"Steve, that might not be the best idea. What if I fell asleep?"

"Just don't go past that buoy right out there. There are tons of people around, and I'll be right here in case anything goes wrong. Just put Ella's life jacket on her."

"Come on, Mommy," Ella says, brightly. "Let's go."

So I put Ella's life jacket on her, and we go to the water's edge. Steve pushes us and our inflated orange boat out onto the lake. I begin to row. Soon, we are rowing alongside other people in their inflated boats.

Ella claps her hands and starts to sing, "Row, row, row your boat, gently down the stream. Merrily, merrily, merrily, merrily, life is but a dream." She laughs.

"Can I try to paddle?" she says.

"Okay, you can try for a minute." I hand her the oars.

She awkwardly drags them through the water. We don't go anywhere.

"Don't push them too deep," I say. "Pull them toward you, and pull equally hard on each side to go forward."

She tries again, unconcerned with really going anywhere. "Sing, with me, Mommy."

I join her. "Row, row, row your boat gently down the stream. Merrily, merrily, merrily, merrily, life is but a dream." And then the world dissolves.

Saturday, March 18, 5:00 a.m., New York

Tony nuzzles up behind me, his groin pressing up against my behind. He kisses my neck. "I want you so bad, baby," he whispers as he begins to lift my nightshirt.

I pull away.

"Cut it out," I say. "I'm serious. Let me sleep."

My heart is full of panic. In California, I am on a boat with my four-year-old daughter, rowing. My daughter doesn't know how to swim. I'm so angry at Tony right now that I can hardly breathe. I turn over and try desperately to fall asleep. If I can fall asleep quickly, everything will be okay. Tony gets up to go to the bathroom, and I close my eyes and breathe deeply. I visualize each of my chakras, imagining a glowing light inside me as I relax each part of my body.

Saturday, March 18, 2:08 p.m., Lake Tahoe

I open my eyes. Ella is across from me, still rowing, and I am in the boat. Everything is all right.

Thank you, God.

"You fell asleep, Mommy," Ella says.

"I know. But you did a good job," I say. And then I look up. We are no longer next to the other boats or swimmers. We have drifted far away. I can still see Steve out on the shore, but just barely. He is reading his book. Damn him—he is supposed to be watching us. Ella's life jacket lies on the floor of the boat next to her.

"Ella Marie! Why did you take off your life jacket? What were you thinking?" I say.

"I don't need it," she says. "I'm a big girl."

"No, Ella, you are not a big girl. You are only four years old. You are still very little, and you are going to put on your life jacket right now. Do you understand me?"

"No!" she says.

"Well then, I'm going to make you put it on." I stand up and lunge for her, and she pulls away, dropping the oars into the water.

"Shit!" I lean over the side of the boat to grab them before we end up stranded out in the water. And as I lean over, the boat tilts violently, tossing Ella into the deep, cold water. She screams. I lean over the edge of the boat and try to grab at Ella, but I miss. When her head appears again, she has drifted farther from the boat. She is eerily silent as she bobs up and down. She must not understand the danger she is in. I prepare to jump into the water after her…and then the world goes black.

Saturday, March 18, 5:13 a.m., New York

Tony has my nightshirt lifted up, and he is pressing himself against me, one hand feeling my breasts, the other releasing himself from his boxer shorts.

"I said no," I say.

"I need you, Angie," he groans. "I didn't think you'd wake up."

"What the fuck?" I say. "You can't just rape me in my sleep."

"I'm not *raping* you, Angie!" he says as he squeezes my nipple. "You're my girlfriend. I love you."

I try to push him off of me. "Just because you love me doesn't make it okay to force me to have sex with you."

He puts the weight of his body on top of me and starts grinding himself against me.

"I'm not forcing you, baby. Come on. You know you like it. You want it just as bad as I do."

I start to cry, really scared now. Scared that I am going to be raped, scared that my little girl is going to drown. And, I realize, scared that I am going to drown too.

"Please," I say. "My daughter is drowning. I need to save her. She's going to die! I need to go back to sleep."

He laughs. "That was just a bad dream, Ang." He pins my arms down with his hands. "You make me so hot!"

"Get off me!" I say, crying. "Please stop, Tony. Stop."

"God, this is hot," he says, roughly pulling my legs apart.

I scream, adrenaline rushing through my body. "Get the fuck off of me, you motherfucker!" And I hit him in the face with my fist so hard I think I might have broken my hand. I hear a popping sound, and his nose gushes hot blood onto my naked chest.

"You bitch!"

"Get out!" I scream at him. "Get out of here!"

He throws his clothes on, his nose still gushing blood, and then grabs a towel, holding it under his nose, and runs toward the door of my apartment.

"You're a crazy fucking bitch!" he says as he slams the door behind him.

I rush out of bed and lock the dead bolt behind him and then lock all the windows. I am shaking violently. I return to the bed, sobbing and shaking, Tony's blood dripping down my chest. I curl up into a fetal position and try to fall back asleep.

"Please, God," I say, crying. "Please, help me. Please, please, please."

Saturday, March 18, 2:20 p.m., Lake Tahoe

I awaken inside the raft, sitting up with a start. "My baby, where's my baby?" I look around frantically, screaming for help. And then I see Steve treading water and holding on to Ella about ten feet from the boat. He sees me and begins swimming toward the raft with her.

"Thank God," I say. "Thank you. Thank you."

Steve swims up to the raft and hands Ella up to me, and then he climbs in beside us.

"I saw her fall in," he says. "She's going to be fine. She actually treaded water the whole time. She is a very brave girl."

Ella crawls over to me and puts her head on my lap. "Grandpa saved me," she whispers.

"What, sweetheart?" I ask her.

"He held me above the water so I could breathe."

I swallow. "Did you see Grandpa, baby?" I say, my eyes tearing up.

She shakes her head in my lap. "No, but I feeled his arms." She puts her thumb back in her mouth.

Steve puts his arm around me, and I cry, clutching at his chest. "You're the only one I love, Steve. It's only ever been you. I'm so sorry, Steve. I'm sorry I forgot that. Please forgive me."

"Shh." He kisses my head. "I was an idiot. I love you."

When I stop crying, Steve jumps into the water and swims us back to shore, dragging the boat behind him. I clutch Ella's wet, chubby little body to me and kiss her over and over again.

Back at the cabin, we take Ella out of her wet bathing suit, put her in her pink footed pajamas, and then tuck our exhausted little girl down for a nap.

"I love you, button," I say to her, kissing her on the tip of her nose.

"I love you, Mommy," she says groggily, clutching her teddy bear.

I am still wearing my bikini with a towel wrapped around my waist. In under three seconds, Steve and I are in our room, and he is pulling the suit off of me and kissing me like he wants to devour me. I feel like I'm drowning and Steve's kisses are my air. I clutch at him, and we fall onto the bed. Steve manages to kick off his board shorts, and then our naked bodies are intertwined. His skin is so smooth and warm. I nuzzle his neck, and I can smell pine trees. And I find that, despite everything that has happened between us these last couple of months, nothing has really changed. We still fit together perfectly. This time, Steve's name is the one I call out.

Later, Steve wraps a coil of my hair around his finger.

"You really scared me today, Angela," he says.

"I know," I say, kissing his fingers. "I was scared too. And, Steve, I'm sorry about the whole Tony thing. I'm sorry I hurt you."

Steve sighs. "I know you are, Angie. And I'm sorry too. I changed the rules on you midgame. I went from 'sure, cutie, date whoever you want in your little dreamland' to 'how dare you cheat on me in your other life?' pretty much overnight. And right after your dad died."

My eyes fill with tears. "Steve, you really understand me. You're the only one who ever has."

Steve pulls his arms tighter around me.

"And if I hadn't ordered you around like I was in charge, maybe your stubborn side wouldn't have kicked in so strong."

I smile. "What stubborn side?"

Steve pinches my left butt cheek. "This side. This one's the stubborn side."

I laugh. "Thank you so much, Steve."

"For what?" he says.

"Being perfect," I say. I hug his arms. "Steve?"

"Yeah?"

"Do you think my dad was really here today? Like Ella said? Do you think he was protecting us?"

"I don't know," Steve says, stroking my arm. "I never believed in angels. But then, I never believed in alternate realities either. I'd say that stranger things have happened."

"Yeah." I smile.

I throw on my pink fuzzy bathrobe (which Ella calls my Muppet robe), and we retrieve Ella from her bed. Then we order pizza with sausage, pesto, and mushrooms and eat ourselves sick while watching a Hayley Mills marathon on the green-tinted television set. I feel so happy that I could burst, my head on Steve's shoulder, my arm around my little girl, watching *The Trouble with Angels*. We are a family again.

Chapter 31

NOT BEING ABLE to drive was ruining my life. Ruining it. Each of my friends had, if not his or her own car, at least the ability to borrow the family car for the evening. I had my bike...and I was only allowed to ride on the sidewalk. Not cool.

In New York, it didn't really matter. None of my friends had a car (or even a license) there. In the city, a car was more of a liability than anything else. You had to navigate through traffic, pay for parking, and deal with trying to find a spot; it was easier just to take a cab or the subway. But in California, anyone who was anyone could drive.

As a junior at Kennedy High, I felt the lack of a license keenly. Though my friends willingly drove me to and from school, weekends were another matter. Due to my narcolepsy and my need for a good night's sleep, I had to be in bed by only eight o'clock. Because of the time difference, going to bed at eight in my Sacramento life still meant I wouldn't wake up until eleven in New York. My New York parents had realized my "narcolepsy" acted up whenever I got up any earlier, so they had arranged for me to be able to do some of my classes as independent study and sleep in late. Of course, here in Sacramento no one was ever willing to leave a party early just to drive me home, so I got picked up by my dad. And usually, my dad would come inside and introduce himself to the kids (meaning that we had to hide all the illegal substances just before he arrived). He liked to stay for upward of twenty minutes, joking around and talking sports with the guys. It was beyond humiliating.

And it wasn't just that. The idea of driving seemed so exciting. I imagined what it would feel like to be in control of this huge machine, hurtling down the freeway, the windows open, the wind in my hair...I couldn't believe I would never get to feel that thrill.

One sunny afternoon in May, my friend Sarah was giving me a ride home from school in her green SUV.

"I'm so jealous of you," I said. "I really wish I could drive, even just one time!"

"Why are your parents so strict?" she said.

"Well, it's because of my narcolepsy. They're scared I'll fall asleep at the wheel."

Sarah laughed. "Yeah, I guess that could be a bit of a problem. I never really see you fall asleep though. Does it really happen that much?"

"No…not that much. Anyway, I think I should at least get to learn how. But my dad is dead set against it."

"I could teach you," she said.

I nearly jumped out of my seat with excitement. "Are you kidding me?"

"I'm not going to let you drive on the freeway or anything, but we could go to an empty parking lot or something. And if you fall asleep, I'll just wake you up."

"I know the perfect spot," I said.

Sarah turned on the radio and began humming to the music. This was it! I was finally going to learn how to drive. I knew my parents would kill me if they found out, but really, what could go wrong? Sarah would be right next to me. She'd wake me up immediately if I fell asleep. And besides, I would be driving really slowly.

A few minutes later, we were parked in a new housing development. No one had moved into the homes yet, so the streets were deserted. It was the perfect place to learn how to drive. My heart racing, with anticipation rather than fear, I switched seats with Sarah.

"Okay," she said, "first, you adjust the rearview mirror. Then, hold your foot down on the break and turn the key in the ignition."

As I did, the car roared to life. This was going to be good.

"Great, now when you're ready, just ease your foot off the brake and hold the steering wheel straight…Ready?"

I nodded.

"Okay, ease your foot off the brake."

Slowly, I lifted my foot from the brake, and the car began to roll forward, glacially.

"Um, can we go a little faster?" I said.

"Okay, you can push a little on the gas—"

Before she had finished the sentence, my foot was on the gas pedal. The car lurched forward. Out of the corner of my eye, I saw Sarah clutch the side of the seat with her hands.

"*Light* pressure, Angela. Light pressure!"

I eased off a bit. Now we were rolling along at a jaunty pace, fast approaching the corner.

"Okay," Sarah said, "now turn the wheel very gently to the right."

This time, I listened to her, turning the wheel just the slightest bit to the right. The SUV rounded the corner. I was driving! I was actually driving.

"This is amazing," I said. "It's like playing a video game!"

Sarah laughed. "Yeah, kind of."

After about a half hour, we ended our little lesson, and Sarah drove me home.

"That was actually really good for your first time, Angie," Sarah said, running her fingers through her long, honey-brown hair. "I would totally let you try real roads if...you know, you weren't narcoleptic."

"Thanks. That was really cool."

After my lesson with Sarah, I couldn't get driving out of my mind. It was so amazing to be in control of that huge SUV. With my unique life, I rarely felt in control of anything. As the days went by, I began scheming about how I could continue to drive. I didn't want to hurt anyone, but I also felt that it was very unlikely that I would fall asleep as long as I was careful about when I drove.

A few weeks later, I was given the perfect opportunity. My parents announced that they would now be going out for date night every Friday evening. Jonathan was already away at college. That meant that I would left behind... along with my mother's car. That evening, after everyone had left the house, I got in the car and turned the ignition. My palms were sweaty. I took a deep breath and slowly eased my foot off the brake. Going about two miles an hour, I drove down my street and then onto Pocket Road. Pocket was pretty busy, and I knew I had to increase my speed. I pushed my foot down on the gas pedal and watched the speedometer slowly rise to thirty. I was driving for real now!

It became my Friday night tradition to go on drives. At first I only drove for about twenty minutes. But after a month, I was going on hour-long drives, always making sure to fill the gas tank to the exact level it was at when I took the car. My parents never suspected anything.

Finally, it was the end of the school year. The seniors were graduating, and there were parties all over town. I decided to go to the party being held at Matt Hoyt's house. There was rumored to be a swimming pool, a billiard table, and copious amounts of liquor. Best of all, it started early, which meant I could actually stay awhile. It sounded perfect.

When I drove up in my mother's Mazda, I could see a few of my friends stop and stare. I got out of the car and walked up the driveway.

"I thought you couldn't drive!" my friend Anna said.

"I can now."

"Cool."

The party was awesome. Matt gave me some beer in a big red plastic cup, and before I knew it, I was pleasantly buzzed. I went swimming (another thing I wasn't supposed to do) and then had a second and a third beer. If I was breaking the rules, I might as well break them! At seven, I knew that I should leave. If not, I risked the possibility of waking up in my other life (and of falling asleep at the wheel).

But as I headed out of the house, I felt the room lurch. I was, most definitely, still tipsy. I weighed my options. I could drive home now, but I knew that driving drunk was never a good idea, especially for someone who didn't even have a driver's license. Or I could wait an hour. No one here was sober enough to drive me home. My only other option was to call my parents. But then I would be grounded for the rest of my life. I decided to wait it out. Over the next hour, I drank a large cup of coffee and several glasses of water. By eight o'clock, I felt fine. And I knew that I couldn't afford to wait any longer to get home.

"Bye!" I said as I slammed the door behind me.

I practically ran to my car. My face felt hot. I breathed deeply. I could do this. I slid into the front seat, slammed the door, and started the car. I only had about a ten-minute drive. I would drive slowly, and everything would be fine. Gingerly, I pulled the car out and turned onto the road, going no more than twenty-five.

The ride went smoothly. Finally, I neared my street. I turned the corner and breathed a sigh of relief…

…And then I woke up in my bed in New York.

"Angie, get up now!" my mom said. "The Taylors are coming for brunch. It's time to get out of bed."

"Just five more minutes, Mom!" I turned over and closed my eyes.

I woke up in the car, my head against the airbag, broken glass surrounding me. My neck hurt so badly. I lifted my head and looked up. The front of the car was completely smashed in…the car was totaled. I had hit my neighbor's tree. But I was alive, although I wouldn't be for long once my parents saw the car.

My mother was shaking me. "Honey, for gosh sakes. I'll get you some coffee, okay?"

"No, Mom." Tears rolled down my cheeks. "I feel really sick. Really nauseated. Can I please just go back to sleep?"

My mother felt my head with the back of her hand. "Hmm…you don't feel warm. But if you feel that sick, maybe you'd better stay in bed."

"Thanks, Mom," I said.

The next thing I knew, I heard sirens.

When my parents found out what I had done, I was put on virtual house arrest. They didn't even trust me to get rides from friends; they were terrified someone might let me behind the wheel again.

But they didn't need to worry, because I had learned my lesson. And I promised myself never to take a stupid risk like that again. I didn't want to die…I just wanted to be normal. But I wasn't normal. And I never would be.

Chapter 32

Saturday, March 18, 12:00 p.m., New York

I AM LYING on my bed, naked, my chest covered in dried blood. Tony's blood. *Oh no.* The events of last night replay themselves in my head, and I feel a wave of nausea wash over me. I run to the toilet just in time to vomit.

Yesterday, in California, all I could think about was how lucky I was. How lucky that I stopped Tony, how lucky that Ella was alive, how lucky that Steve still loved me. But now, looking around my tiny apartment, I feel nothing but hollow. Here, in New York, my life is over. I am apparently such a poor judge of character that I have been dating a rapist for the last six months. I want to kick myself for my stupidity. I can't believe I ever thought I loved him. He didn't really know me. I couldn't even tell him about my other life, because I knew he would reject me if I did. And obviously, I didn't really know him.

I stand up and catch a glimpse of myself in the mirror. My hair is matted to the side of my head, and I have smeared mascara under my eyes. Shaking, I return to my bedroom, rip all of the sheets off of my bed, and throw them into the trash. I take a wet paper towel and wipe up the blood from the floor. Then I turn the shower on as hot as I can stand it, step inside, and just scrub myself with a washcloth. I keep scrubbing long after the blood is gone, my chest pink, trying to wash Tony out of my pores. When my chest starts to turn red, I stop and turn the water off, grabbing a plush green towel and folding myself into it. Suddenly exhausted, I go and lie down on my stripped bed and close my eyes. I know it will mean some major insomnia in California, but I don't care. I would rather be lying awake next to the man I love than having to remain conscious here.

An hour later, I sit up in bed, reach for my phone, and call Jana, who insists on coming over.

When I open the door, I realize that my wrists are covered in purple bruises. Jana follows my gaze.

"Oh my God! He did that to you?"

"I got him worse," I say.

I make a pot of coffee, and while it brews, I tell Jana everything.

"Wait!" Jana says. "He tried to rape you at a restaurant? Why didn't you tell me about that?"

I sigh. "I don't know. It's hard to explain. He did stop when I made it really clear I wanted him to."

"No, no, hold it," she says. "He stopped when you made it clear you were accusing him of trying to rape you."

"Well, but he thought I was just scared of getting caught, not that I didn't want to."

"Look, it doesn't matter whether you said no because you didn't want to or because you were afraid of getting caught. It doesn't matter that he was your boyfriend. The point is, *that time* you said no."

"Yeah, I know," I say, slightly annoyed. "That's all very clear now, but at the time, it wasn't. We hadn't had sex in a long time. My dad was sick…I wasn't thinking clearly. At the time, I believed him when he said he never would have forced me."

"But did you *feel* like he was going to force you?" Jana says quietly.

"Yeah," I say. "Yeah, I did."

Jana stands up. "I'd like to kill him. I really would."

I nod. "Don't think I haven't spent the last half hour thinking of exactly how I'd do it…I actually thought I was in love with him."

"You were thinking of marrying him!"

I hang my head.

"So you really broke his nose?" Jana says, a hint of admiration in her voice.

"Yeah, I think I did," I say. "I heard a definite crack, and his nose bled all over me and the sheets. I woke up covered in his blood."

"I just don't get it! What was he thinking? There was no reason for him to try to do that to you," she says.

"I think he's one of these guys, though, where once you are his girlfriend, he thinks you're his property. Once you've had sex with him, he thinks he has the right to have sex with you whenever he wants."

Jana purses her lips. "Angela, as much as it pains me to say it, I guess at least you found out who he really is. He showed you his true colors before you got married. And you're okay."

"Yeah."

Later, after Jana leaves, I feel alone. Very alone. I keep thinking about how I have a fire escape that leads right into my window and about how very angry Tony was when he left. I feel my face start to tingle. I have to get out of my apartment.

Shortly thereafter, I arrive on the doorstep of my parents' apartment, an overnight bag in hand. My mother opens the door before I knock.

"Uh-oh," she says. "What happened now? You didn't predict anything else, did you?"

I shake my head, tears building up in my eyes.

"You broke up with Tony," she says. I nod. "She broke up with Tony!" my mom calls to my dad.

He appears behind her. "How could anyone break up with you?"

A tear runs down my cheek as I walk into the apartment and set my bag in the living room. "He didn't break up with me. He tried to rape me."

"Oh my word!" my mom says.

My dad's eyes are dark. "I'll kill him!"

"It's okay, Daddy. I'm fine."

"I'm calling the police," my dad says.

"No! Don't. I can't. I know I probably should, but I just don't want to go through all of that. I just want to forget it ever happened. I really am okay."

"Are you sure?"

"Yes," I say, "I'm sure. And actually…I'm pretty sure I broke his nose."

"That's my girl," my dad says.

My mom pulls out a chair for me. "Here, sweetheart, sit down. I'll be right back."

A few moments later, my mom returns with a fresh-from-the-oven, buttered piece of banana bread. She sits beside me and puts her hand on mine, motioning my dad from the room.

"Now tell me what happened, honey."

I take a bite, savoring the warm, soft bread. "Well, Tony woke me up in the night, and he wanted to have sex. I told him to stop, and he just…wouldn't. Not until I punched him. And the thing is that in my…other life, my daughter and I were in the water, in a lake."

My mother shakes her head. "So you were afraid you were going to drown?"

I nod.

"Angie, what do you think would have happened? If you had died…there. Do you think you would have died here too?"

"Maybe…But I don't think so. If I stub my toe here, it isn't stubbed there. I do wonder what will happen though, eventually. I guess I'll find out someday. You want to hear the really weird thing though, Mom? Ella fell out of the boat, and she treaded water until Steve was able to pull her to safety. And she told us that my dad had saved her. She said that he held her above the water so that she could breathe. She couldn't see him, but she felt his arms around her. And she's only four, and she has a pretty active imagination, but it's still pretty amazing."

"That is pretty amazing…I'm just glad you're all right though."

"Me too."

"So, honey," my mom says, picking up a crumb and putting it on the white cloth napkin, "are you worried that Tony will try to contact you again?"

"Yeah," I say. "That's why I'm here."

My mom looks up quickly. "Well, Angie, he knows where we live too!"

"I know he does. But you guys have a doorman. And I already told him not to let Tony up."

"Okay," my mom says, taking my dish to the sink. "But be careful. If he tries anything, you get a restraining order."

"I will."

Later that evening, I am lying on the couch, watching TV, my head on my mom's lap.

"Are you okay, honey?" she says.

"Not really," I say. "I just feel like I have nothing now, except you and Dad. I almost lost my baby because of Tony…I love my husband. I love Steve. I was just fooling myself to think that I could ever marry someone else. There is no one else that I could ever be with, not really. He is the love of my life. It just kills me that he isn't here too, like you are. I miss him so much, and I miss my daughter too." I start to sniffle. "It's not fair, Mom. Why can't I just be normal? Why do I have to be such a freak?"

My mom gives me a hug. "I don't know why you have to live like this. I wish I could make it all better…I think that this is a special gift though. You were able to save your daddy's life with the knowledge you gained there. You're doing more in your life than most people ever can. And just think how lucky you are to have found Steve at all. A lot of people never find a love like that."

I wipe my eyes with the back of my hand. "I know. I know I'm lucky. I just wish that I could have happiness here too. I don't want to be alone forever."

"Well, that's understandable. But I think when you love someone the way you love Steve, anyone you find here would just be second best. You may have two different lives, but you only have one you and one heart and one soul mate. And your soul mate is Steve."

"He is," I whisper.

"I just wish I could meet him," my mom says, squeezing my hand.

That night, I am lying in bed, thinking about my life. Or my lives. The moon is full tonight, and a cool glow shines through my window. Right now I wish I could just escape from this life. Maybe I could take sleeping pills tomorrow and just lie awake and watch Steve sleep. But no, there wouldn't really be a point. I just don't know what to do. I don't want to face Tony. I don't want to do anything except go back to California and stay there. California…maybe I can't spend all of my time in my other life, but there is nothing to stop me from spending all of my time in California. Maybe what I need is a vacation.

Chapter 33

Saturday, March 25, 11:59 a.m. Sacramento

STEVE, MY MOM, and I are taking Ella to the Sacramento Zoo, where a monkey has just given birth. Ella is extremely excited. She has talked about nothing but the baby monkey since she heard about its birth yesterday on the five o'clock news. My little chatterbox. She started talking early and hasn't stopped for air since.

"Mommy, does the monkey have wings?"

"No, Ella," I say, turning on the radio.

"Monkeys don't ever have wings," Steve says, switching into the fast lane.

"They do on *Wizard of Oz*," Ella says.

My mom laughs and leans over to give Ella a hug. "That's true, Ella. But real monkeys don't have wings."

"I want wings," Ella says wistfully. "Also, I want a little doggie that's named Toto. And I want magical red shoes."

At the zoo, we see the pink flamingos standing on one leg, the polar bears, the seals, the cheetah, and finally we battle the crowd in front of the monkey cage. There are signs everywhere: "Quiet please! The new family needs peaceful time to bond." A hush is over the crowd. When we get to the front, Ella gasps, and so do I. The baby monkey is tiny, a sweet furry little thing. And the top of his head is red. On the branch of a tree, he is snuggled in between his mother and father. Steve takes several pictures. When we finally walk away, Ella is skipping and jumping, nearly overloaded by the cuteness of it all.

"I love the monkey! I love him!" she says.

Monday, March 27, 1:00 p.m., New York

"Seats one through twenty-four can now board the plane for flight 291," says the voice through the loudspeaker at JFK.

I stand up, clutching my carry-on luggage, and wait in line. Then I hand the flight attendant my ticket and board the plane. I find my seat and get myself situated, putting my bag under the seat in front of me, spreading the blue fuzzy blanket across my knees and putting the small pillow behind my neck. I feel a great sense of excitement. I've never been to California in this life. I wonder what will be different and what will be the same. I also feel a knot of fear in the pit of my stomach. What if it really upsets me to be in all the familiar places without the familiar people?

I take a deep breath and reassure myself that I have worked everything out perfectly. I recently received a call from Second Stage, asking me to design *110 in the Shade*. I said I would be out of town, but that didn't bother the producers, as long as I could fly back for tech week. And best of all, they put me in touch with an actor from Philadelphia who is coming in to do the show and needed a place to sublet. The actor renting my apartment is very young and very sweet and assured me she would keep everything in perfect condition. I told her she could help herself to my collection of plays and that she shouldn't leave dirty dishes around if she didn't want roaches. Then I handed over the keys.

I hum the tune to "Leaving on a Jet Plane."

Chapter 34

STUDYING ABROAD HAD been both my best and worst semester of college. I loved France and, oddly enough, felt rather at home there. After six years of French classes, I was reasonably fluent enough to get by, and I adored everything French: the art, the cheese, the wine, the cafés, and most especially, the delectable multicourse meals that lasted for hours. The only problem was that Steve, with an unfortunate lack of funds from his parents, had been unable to join me. Thus I had spent my time in France both rhapsodizing over the culture and bemoaning the absence of my American fiancé.

Having an American fiancé had both hampered my time there and sheltered me from the men just hoping to have their shot at an American girl (a species rumored to be sexually undiscriminating when it came to French men).

One night, dancing in a French nightclub, a guy tried to put his hand up my skirt.

"Hey!" I said. "Arrete!"

"Kiss me," he said.

"I'm engaged to someone!"

"Is he in France?"

"No."

"Then it doesn't count," he said, trying to kiss me again.

I managed to push him off of me and run for my life.

After one too many e-mailed accounts of similar encounters, Steve decided to join me for my last two weeks in Paris, using money he had saved over the course of the semester.

When I met Steve at the airport, I threw myself at him, literally jumping off of the ground and wrapping my legs around his waist. We made out there in the terminal, in a way that would have been shocking in America but was merely par for the course in Paris.

"I love you so much," Steve said. "I hope you don't mind, but I decided I'm not going to break physical contact with you for the next two weeks."

I laughed. Seeing Steve in the flesh after almost five months apart was oddly eerie. His physical presence was somehow different than I had remembered. He seemed almost like a wax figure in a museum. I shook my head, sure I was really beginning to lose it. This was just Steve…my Steve.

The sudden intimacy after all this time felt even odder. I almost felt like I needed to have a long conversation with him before I'd feel comfortable walking hand in hand again. *Ridiculous*, I admonished myself, nestling under his arm as we went to find a taxi.

I soon realized, however, that the slight distance I felt was due to the fact that I had experienced so much that he had not. I was used to him knowing every intimate detail of my life. But here, he did not. So over the course of the next two weeks, I set about showing him. I introduced him to the unparalleled joy that was a profiterole from the pâtisserie around the corner from my dorm. I took him to Notre Dame, to the Louvre, to the Seine…

On our last day in France, I took Steve to the Musée d'Orsay, my favorite place in Paris, all marble and light and beautiful swirling pastel paintings and white statues. As we walked through the museum, hand in hand, I had the feeling that for one of the first times of my life, I was exactly where I wanted to be most in the world, with the person I most wanted to be with.

"Steve," I said, "isn't this just the perfect moment?"

A shaft of late-afternoon sunlight illuminated the right side of his face.

"Yeah. I kind of wish I'd waited to propose."

"I'm really glad you came. France just wasn't the same without you here."

"I'm glad I came too," he said. "Now I understand why you fell in love with Paris."

"Did you fall in love too?"

"With Paris or with you?" he said, squeezing my hand.

"Both," I said.

"Both."

"I wish we never had to leave," I said, wrinkling my brow. "I like it here so much more than America."

"Me too. Let's move," Steve said recklessly.

I looked up at him, my eyes wide. "Why not? Steve, we both speak the language; we love it here. We don't own a house or have kids. What's to stop us? Why don't we really move here?"

Steve rubbed his chin. "Oh, Ang, I don't know…I wasn't really being serious. I'd love to live here, but I don't know if I'd want to be so far from my family. I don't know if I'd really want to raise kids here one day. They would be French, and we wouldn't be, really, and it would be…weird."

"Maybe," I said. "But maybe it wouldn't be permanent. Just a few years. It would be an adventure…we'd never forget it."

Steve nodded. "Let's think about," he said.

And we did think about it. But in the end, it seemed impractical. France was expensive and far away, and we didn't have jobs there. So we stayed in California. Of course, that didn't mean that I didn't sometimes cook up a soufflé that we could eat by candlelight, professing our love in French.

Chapter 35

Tuesday, March 28, 8:30 a.m.—visit to Sacramento

YESTERDAY, I ARRIVED in Sacramento at around four o'clock California time and then took an Uber to my hotel. After checking in, I ordered some pizza and then read until bedtime.

After a brief hiatus in my other life, I woke up feeling refreshed and as though it was three hours later than the red glowing numbers on the clock told me it was. Now, after a quick shower, I sit looking out the window. I decide to spend the day enjoying myself, walking around Land Park, shopping at some thrift stores, and catching a movie at the downtown plaza. On a whim, I decide to go to a classical concert I saw advertised in the lobby. This is an unheard of luxury in my normal life in Sacramento. Steve and I used to go to concerts, before Ella was born. But now the closest thing I get to the symphony is listening to Beethoven in the car.

In the concert hall, I listen rapturously as the orchestra transports me to other times and places. I find myself remembering my early days with Steve, listening to CDs in his dorm room. I realize, with a smile, that I have hardly thought of Tony at all. That is, until this moment. I banish him from my thoughts, turning my attention instead to the musicians. I notice a beautiful blond woman, her hair pulled back in a bun. And then, next to her, a familiar broad-shouldered man...Steve! My heart starts to race. But no, it can't be him. This man has longer hair, is thinner. I wish I was closer and could get a better look. I squint. And then as surely as I know my own reflection, I know that it is him. I had never dared to hope that he could be here, in this life, and yet here he is. When the performance is over, I stand outside the stage door and wait. I don't know what I am waiting for exactly; I don't know if I should speak to him. I just know that I have to get a better look at him. As the musicians begin to file out, waving good night to each other, I feel my heart race in anticipation. And then there he is. Steve. I look at him and catch his eye, and for a just a moment, I feel like he recognizes me. But then he keeps walking. I turn and begin walking back to my hotel, feeling a heaviness in my chest. What had I expected to happen? This Steve doesn't even know me. And he never will. I decide to walk a bit more around downtown, unwilling to go to bed just yet. I end up walking toward the lawn of the capitol and eventually sitting on a bench. I look down at my nails. They are uneven. I pick at my cuticles, wondering if I should just head back to New York. Suddenly, I hear Steve's voice.

"Excuse me, but didn't I see you at the symphony tonight?"

I look up. Steve is standing there, wearing jeans and a baseball cap, walking a golden retriever. I laugh, not quite believing that I am really talking to Steve. My Steve. But here.

"Yes. You were wonderful," I say.

"Thanks."

Steve's golden retriever trots over to me and lays his head on my lap.

"Sorry. I think he must like you."

"That's okay," I say. "He's a sweetheart." I pat him on the head. "What's your name?"

"I'm Steve."

I smile. "I was actually talking to the dog."

He laughs. "Oh, of course. His name is Buddy."

"Nice to meet you, Buddy," I say. "I'm Angela."

"So, Angela, are you new to the neighborhood?"

I shrug. "Sort of. I'm here in Sacramento on vacation."

He looks intrigued. "Where are you from?"

"New York."

"New York City?"

"Yeah. I'm a costume designer."

"What a cool job."

"Your job is pretty cool too."

For a moment, we lock eyes, and I feel that connection, the one that told me I belong with this man, years ago in college. He looks like he feels the same connection.

I can see that he is nervous. He would probably appear confident to anyone else. But I know that when Steve is nervous, he stands up really straight and looks very serious. It takes a moment for me to connect the fact that he must be nervous to be talking to me. After all these years, it is so strange to think that I could make Steve nervous.

"Listen…would you, uh, like me to maybe show you around town a little? I've lived here a long time." He looks at me expectantly.

"Sure, that would be really great. When would you like to do it?" *Do it?* What kind of an idiot says *do it*? I'm blushing, which is even more embarrassing than the fact that I said "do it," because now he knows exactly what I was thinking.

Steve holds back a little smile. "How about Saturday?" he says. "I can come pick you up around one o'clock. Where are you staying?"

I tell him I'm staying at the Hyatt. "I'll see you Saturday, then."

I nod, speechless.

Chapter 36

Wednesday, March 29, 12:30 p.m., Sacramento

Ella and I arrive at Sutterville Preschool. Again, it is my day to help out at Sutterville, and I am wishing with all of my heart that it wasn't. I sigh. I could really use the break from Ella for a few hours as well as the chance to get a little time to myself. I wouldn't mind sitting down and reading some articles or even, wonder of wonders, a book. And not one I read on my phone while Ella watches TV. A big, real book, the kind Ella is prone to grabbing from my hands and trying to "read," ensuring I don't get to. Before I had a child, I used to often read a book in a day. Now, I am lucky if I get through four chapters over the course of four months.

Being a mother is harder than I ever thought it would be. I love Ella more than anything, and I cherish her even more now that I almost lost her. I don't blame her for being a kid and needing peanut butter and jelly and story time and all the other things kids need. I just wish that Steve was around more. Weekends and evenings are nice. He loves Ella and spends lots of time with her. And when she was a baby, he got up with her every night, which I am eternally grateful for. But now that Ella is older, it seems like it's always me who has to meet her needs. I'm always the one who does the cooking, the cleaning, the bathing, the comforting...And sometimes I get a little burned out.

Today, I am assigned to the cooking station. Ella immediately starts to cry. The parents who prepare the snack have to work in the kitchen, where the children are not allowed.

One of the other moms shoots me a sympathetic glance.

"Elly, it's okay," I say. "This will be just like a day when I'm not here. You go and play with the other kids, do a craft, and then at snack time I'll sit next to you. Okay?"

She sticks her lip out at me. "No, I wanna sit by you now!"

"Young lady," I say, wincing as I realize that I sound like my own mother, "you cut out that whining. I'm going to take you over there to play with the Play-Doh."

I hold out my hand to her, and to my utter surprise and horror, instead of taking my hand, she bites it.

"Ow!" I say. "Ella! That was very, very naughty! You tell Mommy that you are sorry."

"No!" she says.

The other mother looks away.

"Ella, I mean it! Say sorry." She doesn't respond.

"Okay," I say, walking toward her. "Then it's time for a time-out."

Hearing this, Ella turns around and bolts out of the kitchen. I debate whether to chase her out there, drag her inside, and give her a time-out, or whether to simply let it go. Just at that moment, Miss Nishamura walks over to me to check in and see what I'm preparing. By the time she has left, I see that Ella is playing on the swings with her friends, laughing and smiling. I decide not to deal with her right now, but I resolve that we will have a long discussion about not biting when we get home this afternoon.

I set to work making the snack. I have to make thirty mini blueberry muffins, apples with sun nut butter (no peanut butter allowed), and a whole assortment of cut-up raw vegetables. In silence, I chop carrots as the other mother cuts up construction paper for her craft. I feel so embarrassed by what happened. I hate to look like a parent who can't control her own kid, especially because I usually do pretty well. She just caught me off guard with the biting. I sigh, louder than I mean to.

The other mother looks at me and grins. Every part of her is long and thin: her legs, her torso, even her face. She doesn't wear any makeup, but she has attractive features, clear blue eyes, and dirty-blond hair pulled back into a tight ponytail.

"You've got a little hell-raiser just like my son, I see."

I nod, glad that she can understand what I'm dealing with. "Yep. The worst part is that she refuses to say she's sorry. No matter what she's done, no matter what punishment she receives, she absolutely refuses to say she's sorry."

"Well," the other mother says, "maybe she's not sorry."

I laugh. "You may have hit on something there. I'm Angela, by the way." I hold out my hand. "Just don't bite it," I say.

"Don't worry," she says, shaking my hand. "I won't. I'm Becca Ferris. Jayden's mom. We're new here."

"Oh, he's a cutie." I add a handful of carrot sticks to a platter.

"Thanks. So is your daughter. He's a handful though. And it's hard, because I'm a single mom. I've got to be mom and dad, you know?"

I shake my head. "Wow, I can't even imagine. I have a good babysitter, if you'd like her number," I say.

Becca eats a carrot stick. "Actually, he stays at my mom's in the evening while I work. I just feel so guilty because it's like I want to spend time with him when I'm at work, but then when I'm at home, I just want a little time to myself."

"Does he ever go to his dad's?" I say.

Becca gnaws on a piece of celery. "Nope. He was deployed, and then when he got back, Jayden was already born. And he was just so not ready to be a dad. He got really screwed up over there. Seriously screwed up. So, whatever. He left. He's living in South America or something. I don't even know. We don't talk."

I take out a bowl and pour in the blueberry muffin mix. "I'm sorry." It feels so inadequate, but I don't know what else to say.

"Yeah, well, I was stupid and in love. I ended up having to drop out of school, start waitressing full time. I do still take classes, but only once a week on Wednesday nights, so it's pretty slowgoing. Not that I would give up Jayden for anything. It's just that the circumstances could have been more ideal."

"Sure," I say. "Of course." I like Becca. "Hey, would you like to come over sometime and have a playdate with the kids? It could be fun for us too."

Becca grins. "Yeah, you know what? I'd like that. I kind of stopped doing anything fun after Jayden came along. My friends are all still single, and they just don't really get what it's like."

An hour later, we bring the snacks out on trays to the kids. I sit by Ella, who is suddenly demure and well behaved.

"Hey, Ella, how would you like it if Jayden came over to play?" I say.

Ella's eyes light up. "Jayden knows how to do a handstand!" she says.

After the snack, Becca and I make a date to get together next week. And I suddenly feel so much better. I realize that it's been a long time since I really had a friend.

Saturday, April 1, 1:25 p.m.—visit to Sacramento

Steve and I are eating at The Firehouse, a restaurant in Old Sacramento. In my other life, I've been to The Firehouse many times. Here though, I have to pretend that I'm seeing it for the first time. I take in the cobblestone streets, the raised wooden sidewalks, the river…I love Sacramento, and I enjoy seeing it as if for the first time.

"I'm really glad you agreed to go out with me," Steve says. "I have to admit, I didn't think I had a chance. I mean, you're this gorgeous, successful New York woman, and I'm this geeky musician who needs a haircut."

I want to laugh, but don't. In my Sacramento reality, I'm lucky if my husband can make time in his schedule to take me out on a date. This Steve was worried I wouldn't want to go. And he thinks I'm gorgeous. I take a sip of my iced tea.

"You didn't need to worry. I was hoping you'd ask me out."

Steve takes a bite of his tuna tartare. "Why?"

"Well, you just seem like a really nice guy. And you have a cool dog."

He laughs. "Oh, I get it now. You're just using me to get to Buddy, aren't you?"

"You caught me," I say, throwing my hands up. I take a bite of steak, and when I look up, Steve is staring at my mouth. I wonder if I have food stuck in my teeth.

"What?" I say.

"Oh, sorry. I didn't mean to stare…You are just so beautiful."

"Thanks," I say, suddenly shy.

After we finish eating, Steve puts his arm around my waist, and we walk around Old Sacramento. We go into Evangeline's and look at all the costumes, pranks, knickknacks, and movie memorabilia. I walk up to a rack of tricks: gum that turns your mouth blue, cigarettes that squirt water, and rubber cat poop. Then I notice a section of old film noir movie posters.

"Hey, Steve, just look at all these cool posters. I love film noir."

His fingers graze my hip. "Really? I am obsessed with film noir. That's amazing." He picks up a poster of *Double Indemnity*, which I know is his favorite movie.

"That's my favorite movie," I say, and he looks at me like he wants to kiss me.

After he buys the poster, we leave the store, and he hands the bag to me.

"A little souvenir for you," he says. "Hey, let's get our picture taken."

He leads me into a little shop, where I am given a huge saloon-girl dress and he is given a suit. We change into our costumes and get our picture taken, holding a bottle of whiskey and a shotgun. We leave with a wild west–style sepia-colored picture of the two of us.

Afterward, we explore the little one-room schoolhouse and the Delta King, a big paddle boat. I tell him about my childhood, growing up in New York and about college and my career. He also fills me in on his history, and I marvel to discover that his past sounds exactly as I know it from my husband, the one major difference being that he chose to study music instead of architecture...And that, up until now at least, he hasn't known me.

"So," he says, leading me up the ramp from the ship so that we can walk along the river, "why the need for an extended vacation? And why Sacramento?"

I sigh. How do I explain this?

"Oh, it's a long story. I've been really stressed out lately. My dad had lung cancer, and he had to have surgery and chemo, and I've been helping take care of him. He's going to be okay now though. And I also just broke up with someone, and I'm kind of afraid of him, so I thought maybe getting out of town wouldn't be such a bad idea. I'd never been here, and...I thought it might be a nice, quiet place to go to get away."

"Are you okay?" he says, looking concerned. "This ex-boyfriend, he isn't following you or anything, is he?"

I shake my head. "No, nothing like that. I just didn't want to run the risk of seeing him anywhere right now, because I'm not sure how he would react. But he isn't stalking me or anything. Don't worry."

Steve looks relieved.

"So have you dated anyone recently?" I say.

He looks out over the river, which is glistening in the light as the sun just begins to set. "Not too recently. I haven't dated much the last couple of years. Before that, I was engaged, but my fiancée decided that she never wanted to have kids…and that was just a deal breaker for me. She also didn't like dogs. I got Buddy when we broke up."

He takes my hand. "I'm glad you like dogs."

"Me too," I say. "And the no-kids thing would have been a deal breaker for me too."

Steve turns to me, and again I can feel his gaze on my lips. "I'm sorry, Angela, but all day the only thing I've been able to think about is kissing you."

"You don't have to apologize for that," I whisper.

And then he pulls me to him and kisses me on the lips, softly at first and then more urgently. We kiss for a long time, the smell of my vanilla perfume wafting in the air around us. We kiss until I start to shiver in the cool evening breeze. Steve pulls away.

"I could kiss you all evening," he says, nuzzling me with his chin, his stubble scratching my smooth cheek. "But I guess I'd better get you home before you freeze."

In the car, driving back toward my hotel, Steve puts his hand on my knee. "How long are you in town, Angela?" he says.

"Probably at least a month. I'm not sure yet, exactly."

"Good," he says. "I hope that you'll let me continue on as your tour guide. I'd really like to spend some more time with you."

"Of course," I say, looking out at the state capitol shining brightly in the moonlight. "I would love for you to show me around here."

I couldn't stop smiling if I wanted to.

Chapter 37

I WAS JOLTED awake by a terrible pain in my pelvis, like I had the worst menstrual cramps ever.

I grabbed Steve's arm, shaking him awake.

"What is it?" he said, blinking.

This was all wrong. I was only five months along; I wasn't supposed to go into labor. Not yet.

"Are you sure? Maybe you just have gas."

"No, no...I'm having contractions."

Steve sat up in bed and reached for the phone on his nightstand. "I'll call Dr. Rodriguez," he said.

Within twenty minutes, Steve swung our car into the parking lot of the emergency room.

"Stay here. I'll be right back," he said.

He returned with a wheelchair.

"It's okay," I said. "I—

"Just get in."

Steve wheeled me into admissions. I listened while he explained the situation. I felt numb. *Please, God, don't let this baby die.*

Before I knew what was happening, I had been wheeled into an examining room. This must really be dangerous. I'd never gone to the emergency room and gotten seen without waiting for hours.

A young, brunette doctor examined me. She had kind eyes.

"Mrs. Stewart, you've gone into premature labor. But at five months, we need to try to keep your baby from arriving. If you have her now, there is very little chance that she'll survive."

I caught Steve's eye, and his fear was visible. He squeezed my hand.

"I'm going to administer some drugs to try to halt the labor. You'll have to go on complete bed rest. We need to keep you from delivering for as long as possible."

My head was swimming. I could hardly make sense of what I was being told.

"Bed rest?"

I couldn't believe this was happening. Up until now, my pregnancy had gone perfectly. I'd been sick at first, but that had gone away, and I'd been feeling strong and healthy. This was all wrong.

"Steve..." My voice broke.

"It's okay, Angie. We'll get through this together."

Over the next couple of weeks, I was truly confined to my bed. Steve took care of me as much as possible, and I worked on my laptop so that I could continue to meet my deadlines. My parents came by every few days. Other than that, I had nothing to do but watch TV and wait. The waiting was the worst. Part of me wanted this to all be over as soon as possible. I yearned to get out of bed, to resume my life, even just to go to the grocery store. But at the same time, I knew that the longer I was in bed, the better it was for my baby. For Ella. Steve and I had only just settled on a name before I was put on bed rest. I couldn't allow myself to picture the little baby I was going to have; I was too afraid I would lose her.

Then, when I was a mere thirty-three weeks along, it happened. The contractions started, and no amount of medication would stop them. The baby was coming, and she was coming today.

"Steve," I said, "I'm so scared."

"It will be okay, Angie. No matter what happens, it will be okay."

He kissed me.

And then it seemed like things moved at the speed of lightning. Before I knew it, the doctor was telling me that my baby was in distress and that I would have to have a C-section. None of this was going the way I wanted it to. I cried and clutched Steve's hand.

"Now hold perfectly still," the doctor said. "You're going to feel a pinch."

I leaned on the nurse as the needle was put into my back, between my vertebrae. It hurt, but soon, I couldn't feel a thing from the neck down. It was a terrifying feeling. Steve saw the panic in my eyes.

"Just look at me, honey," he said. "Look into my eyes."

"I love you," I whispered.

The doctors had erected a sheet so that I couldn't see them cut me open, but I could feel a tugging, and I knew they were cutting through my skin with a scalpel. I shuddered and concentrated on Steve.

"And...here she is," the doctor said.

Tears spilled from my eyes. "Can I hold her?"

"I'm so sorry, dear," an older nurse said. "She's got to go to the NICU immediately."

I caught a glimpse of my baby as she was whisked from the room. My baby. I started to cry now, uncontrollably. Steve stroked my hair.

Once I had recovered from the surgery, I spent all of my time in the NICU. I refused to go home. I could hardly eat, hardly sleep; I couldn't work at all. Steve came every day after work, and it was only because of him that I went home to sleep. Thankfully, bit by bit, Ella grew stronger.

One day, we stood there together, looking at her through the glass.

"I quit my job today," I said.

"What?"

"Ella is all I care about. I don't want to miss a moment of being her mommy."

Steve bit at a hangnail. "Are you sure, Angie? You love your job. I'm worried that you are just upset right now with Ella in the hospital. You may regret quitting your job when she gets stronger."

"No!" I shook my head violently. "No, Steve. This made me understand what's really important to me. I'm not going back to work. We can afford to live on your income. It will be okay."

Steve smiled, his eyebrows turned down. "I know it will be okay. If this is what you really want, it's fine with me."

"It is what I want."

The day I finally got to hold Ella was the happiest moment of my life. The happiest moment, in fact, of both of my lives.

Chapter 38

Sunday, April 2, 6:25 p.m., Sacramento

STEVE IS BARBEQUING hamburgers in the backyard, and I'm standing beside him, while Ella plays on her swing set. I can't stop thinking about my date with Steve yesterday, about how he kissed me. I just want more. I glance mischievously at my husband.

"Hey, do you want to have a quickie upstairs while those burgers cook?"

Steve looks at me like I'm crazy. "Ella's right here. She'll follow us upstairs."

I sigh, knowing he is right.

"Sorry, you just look so cute with that chef apron on." I press myself against him and kiss him on the lips.

Steve pulls away. "Honey, I'm trying to barbeque."

I shake my head and turn to walk away.

"Come on, babe. Don't be mad," he says. "I love you. This just isn't the time. Maybe tonight, okay?"

"Yeah, okay, sorry," I say.

"What's gotten into you today, hon?"

I smile. "Oh, I just had a really hot date with you last night, that's all."

Steve raises his eyebrow. "With me, huh? What do you mean?"

"Well," I say, putting my arms around him, "in my other life, I decided to take a little vacation to California. And...I found you. The other version of you."

Steve raises his eyebrow. "Are you serious?"

"Completely. I hope this doesn't weird you out too much. I didn't plan it or anything, but once I saw you, I just had to get to know you. And so now we're sort of...dating."

He frowns and considers this for a few moments. "So…what am I like, there?"

"Well, you live in midtown, you play the bass, and you have a golden retriever. You also think I'm really hot."

Steve laughs. "Well that makes two of us." He flips a burger. "This is very surreal, though, isn't it? I mean, isn't it weird for you?"

"It is, yeah. But…you said I wasn't allowed to date anyone except you, right?" I smile.

Wednesday, April 5, 3:45 p.m., Sacramento

"It's just hard because he's starting to ask about it," Becca says.

We are sitting on a park bench together, watching our kids play on the jungle gym.

"What do you tell him?" I ask.

Becca suddenly stands up. "Jayden!" she says. "I am serious. Do not climb up the slide. You could get hurt. Slide down on your butt!" She sits back down and continues as if there had been no interruption. "Well, I usually just say that I don't know where his dad is. But that isn't really working anymore."

I nod sympathetically. I can't even imagine what it would be like to have to try to raise Ella without Steve, not to mention having to try to explain to her where her daddy is.

"Could you just tell him you think his dad is somewhere in South America? That's the truth, right?"

Becca takes out a juice box and hands it to me. "Thirsty?"

"Sure," I say, taking it from her and punching the straw through the foil hole. "Thanks."

"No problem. Anyway, yeah, sure I can tell him his dad is in South America, but I don't know how to answer the rest of his questions. Why doesn't daddy call? Why doesn't daddy send presents on his birthday? Why didn't daddy want him? I don't want to lie to him, but what am I supposed to say?" Her eyes fill with tears, and she brushes them away with her sleeve.

I look down at my juice box. I feel so guilty that my life is so much easier than hers.

"So do you think you might ever go back to work, now that Ella's older?"

"I don't know," I say. "I'm not sure I'm ready for all the responsibility yet. I still really have my hands full with her right now. I do miss writing though."

"So why don't you write, then?" Becca says.

"Oh, I'm way too busy. I'm with Ella every second. It'll probably be years before I have time for stuff like that."

Becca frowns.

"What is it?" I say.

"Well, don't take this the wrong way, but I think you just have to make time if it's important to you. I work, and Jayden is reasonably well adjusted. I think Ella would deal if you took a small amount of time to write."

"Maybe you're right."

After the kids have gotten thoroughly dirty at the park, Becca and Jayden come over to our house for a snack. I take a few fresh avocados from the fruit bowl and slice them open to make guacamole. Becca switches on the television.

And then I recognize the voice I hear. I look up at the TV screen and almost cut through my hand in my excitement.

"Ahh! I know her!"

Becca looks startled. "Who, the girl on the commercial?"

"Yeah," I say, wiping my hands on a kitchen towel. "She's a good friend of mine. How cool!" I excitedly pick up the phone and call Mandy's number, one of the few I know by heart. I am so happy for her. I can't even believe it. The phone rings.

"Hello?"

"Mandy, congratulations! I just saw you on the Crest commercial. That is so amazing for you. I'm so happy."

There is a pause, and then Mandy says, "I'm sorry. Who is this?"

It is then that I realize my mistake. What an idiot. Mandy doesn't know me in this life.

I hang up the phone, blushing, and take out a bowl.

"She didn't remember you?" Becca says.

I laugh it off. "I guess I called the wrong number."

I feel so stupid. Over the years, I have sometimes called the homes of my friends in my other life just to see who answers. It's never been anyone I've known before. How crazy that Mandy actually has the same cell phone number in this life.

"Where do you keep the chips?" Becca says.

"In the pantry, to your left."

I crush the avocados and add lemon juice, paprika, salt, and cayenne pepper, while Becca sets out a bowl of chips.

"Kids, come and have a snack!" I say.

We spend the next hour talking and laughing. Best of all, our kids seem to have hit it off as well as we have.

Later that night, I watch TV alone, waiting for Steve to come home. His hours have been creeping later and later. I know he isn't purposely avoiding me, but he just gets so wrapped up in his work. At almost eight o'clock, he calls and says he'll be several hours yet. I decide to go to bed alone. Again. On the way to bed, I grab one of Ella's stuffed animals, a penguin. At least it will be something to hug.

Chapter 39

Sunday, April 9, 4:39 p.m.—visit to Sacramento

STEVE CALLED ME today to tell me that *Double Indemnity* is playing at the Crest Theater. Steve doesn't know that the two of us have watched this particular movie together countless times. Still, I really don't mind watching it with him again. Since we met, Steve and I have gone on some really wonderful dates and talked on the phone a lot. Often, when I get back to my hotel room, Steve will call a few minutes later just to tell me what a great time he had. It's so cute. I can't help being reminded of my early days with my husband in college. The two of us used to talk on the phone late into the night, even though we'd seen each other earlier the same evening. Sometimes, I would fall asleep with the phone in my hand, and my roommate would have to hang it up for me.

Now, Steve and I are sitting inside the movie theater together. It feels so right to me, having been to the movies with Steve more times than I can possibly count. Still, it somehow feels new and exciting, just knowing that this Steve has never sat next to me in a movie theater before. When the lights go out, Steve reaches for my hand, and I feel like I'm back in college, sitting with Steve at the Holiday Cinema in Davis. I feel an overwhelming happiness inside as I settle against Steve and lean my head on his shoulder. He puts his arm around me, and it feels perfect.

After the movie is over, we go out to dinner at the Empress Tavern. It's fun talking to Steve, sharing my New York life with him. It feels so good to tell him about my life as a costume designer, about my parents, my friends, and New York City, and to have him accept all of it as fact. Of course, I leave out details about my California life, about my dad dying and about my marriage and child. After a few glasses of wine, I start to feel the alcohol hitting me. Steve seems a little bit drunk himself.

"Angie," he says, looking deep into my eyes, "you are the most beautiful woman in the world."

I giggle, and he kisses me, pulling me close.

"I love…" I stop myself just in time. "I love…life."

"You are the perfect woman. Just perfect." He kisses me on the nose, just like my Steve always does.

"Oh, trust me. I'm far from perfect."

"Really?" he says, grinning. "So what's the matter with you? You might as well tell me now."

I bite my lip, wondering if I really should tell him. I decide to go with the sanitized version. "Uh…actually I'm narcoleptic," I say. "So I often fall asleep at slightly inappropriate moments." I look down at my glass. "Sometimes it actually puts my life in danger."

Steve looks at me sympathetically. "That must be so hard." He hugs me tight. "But look at the full life you live anyway. You are a really brave woman."

I lean my head against him. "I guess so. But I'm tired of having to be brave all the time."

Steve pulls back away, his hands on my shoulders. "I'll take care of you."

And I know that this isn't just a line said by a drunk guy in a bar. I know that he really will take care of me.

We leave the bar and walk back to the Hyatt, the cool evening air blowing my skirt around my legs.

"I'll walk you in," Steve says, his hand around my waist.

We take the elevator to the fifth floor, and Steve walks me to the door of my room. In the hallway, he pulls me against him and kisses me deeply.

"You smell like an angel," he whispers. I want him so much. And…after all, he is my husband. But it is already almost eight o'clock, and of course since I am now no longer dealing with a time change, I need to get to bed in order to wake up at eight in my other life. And I am afraid to risk having this Steve sleep in the same bed with me. At least, not until he really understands the consequences. I pull away.

"Listen, Steve," I say, gently. "I really need to get to bed. I'm tired."

He looks at me longingly. "Sure, yeah, no problem. Maybe I could come in just for a minute?"

I sigh. "Well, the truth is, I'm not quite ready."

"Oh. Okay." He smiles sheepishly. "Well, I had a great time. And I really, really like you. I'll call you soon, okay?"

"Sure," I say, kissing him one last time. Then I put my card key in the door, wait for the blinking green light, and step inside my hotel room, leaving Steve in the hallway. I sigh, take a cold shower, and go to bed.

Tuesday, April 11, 5:00 p.m.—visit to Sacramento

Since I have been here in Sacramento, Steve has been showing me around to all of the tourist attractions. I've been having the best time going to all of these places that I rarely have time to go to in my California life. We've gone to Sutter's Fort, the Crocker Art Museum, the state capitol, the governor's mansion, and the Train Museum, where a re-created old passenger train shook as we walked through it. We're having so much fun together. I laugh at Steve's jokes, and we just "get" each other in a way that I never felt with Tony.

Steve is different. When he says he is going to call at seven, he calls at seven on the dot. When he promises to be somewhere, he is there. Steve speaks from the heart. When he tells me I am beautiful, I know that he isn't doing it so that I find him charming. He's saying it because he is truly thinking in that moment that I am beautiful. None of this is new to me. I have seen it all in my Sacramento husband. I just have never experienced it in another man.

I never anticipated the giddy excitement of new love with a man who isn't exactly new to me. When I am with Steve, he makes me want to be a better person, while at the same time making me feel like I already am an amazing person. When I was with Tony, I continually felt the need to strive for his love and acceptance. I felt like I was never quite good enough.

Now, Steve and I are walking Buddy through the Land Park area, among all the big, shady trees and the old, statuesque homes. I pat Buddy on the head.

"You're a good boy," I say.

He pants and looks as though he is smiling at me.

We walk in silence for a while, just enjoying each other's presence. Steve puts his arm around me.

"I love you, Angela," he says.

I stop and look at him, at the one man whom I have loved since my teens. I can hardly believe that this is happening.

"Really?" I whisper.

"Really."

"I love you too."

And I feel tears begin to pool in my eyes. It seems almost too good to be true, that this should really be happening to me after all I've been through.

"Don't cry," he says, wiping a tear away with his finger.

Buddy looks back at us, as if to say, *Hey, guys, c'mon. Why are we just standing here?* We laugh and continue walking.

"Steve," I say, "how can you know you love me when you've known me such a short time?"

"I don't know," he says. "The thing is, I feel like I've known you forever. I know it sounds weird and maybe a little cheesy, but I feel like you understand me in a way that no one ever has in my life. Almost like you can read my mind sometimes. You just dropped out of nowhere and came into my life and…now I can't imagine my life without you."

"Oh, Steve…"

I want to tell him everything, but I can't. Not yet. I waited quite a while until I told my husband about my other life. I was worried he would think I was crazy, but he didn't, not really. He just thought I was cute and quirky and that I had an active imagination. But I'm not a nineteen-year-old girl anymore. My story might not sound quite as cute and quirky coming from a thirty-year-old woman.

"I feel the same way as you do," I say.

Steve holds my hand tightly in his. "Angie…" He shakes his head. "I know I'm getting ahead of myself here, but you leave soon. What do we do then? I don't want to lose you. I can't even think about it. It's too sad."

I sigh. "I don't know. I guess we can visit each other and talk on the phone a lot."

"Yeah, I know," he says, "but long term that won't work. And you can't leave New York really. You need to be there for your career. I won't let you give all that up for me. But then, I can't really imagine living in New York City."

Suddenly, I feel a cold chill run down my spine. And I realize that this perfect moment, this beautiful walk, these heartfelt emotions, are all just leading up to the kindest dumping I've ever received.

"So you want to break up when I leave then," I say flatly.

Steve looks shocked. "Oh no, that wasn't—no, I really don't want to break up. You don't want to, do you?"

I link my arm in his. "No, no, I don't at all."

"Good," he says. "Listen—I was just thinking ahead and realizing that we'll have some tough choices to make. But I want to make this work. I promise you that I'll do my best to make this work."

"So will I."

We go back to Steve's place to watch *Roman Holiday*. On the couch, I lean into him, and he takes my face in his hands and kisses me on the lips, gently but urgently.

"Do you want to stop the movie?" he whispers. "I can't think about anything except you anyway. I want to kiss every inch of you."

His breath is warm on my neck, and suddenly I want him so badly, and I can hardly believe I've held out this long. But now there is no reason not to. I trust him completely. I know that he would never, ever hurt me. And he loves me.

"Stop the movie," I say.

Steve pushes Stop on the remote, turns off the TV, and then leans me back on the couch and lies on top of me, covering me with kisses. He pulls off my dress and his shirt, and it feels so good to just be here with him, naked, and to feel so safe and secure. His body is a little different than my husband's, a bit slimmer, but otherwise the same old Steve.

"God, I need you Angie," he moans.

Then I feel someone licking my toes. And it isn't Steve. I scream, and Steve jumps back. Buddy is licking my toes with his big, fat, slobbery tongue.

"Hey, Buddy," Steve says. "This is *my* girl."

He picks me up and carries me into his bedroom and closes the door. It is my second first time with Steve, only this time neither one of us are virgins.

Afterward, I lie in his arms and know that the universe has finally righted itself. This is where I am meant to be. Steve strokes my thigh.

"Stay with me tonight," he whispers, his breath tickling my ear.

"I will."

Chapter 40

Thursday, April 13, 3:10 p.m., Sacramento

"MOMMY, WHAT NUMBER is next after one hundred?"

I am on the bus with Ella, bringing her home from Sutterville. While I am incredibly proud of my smart little girl for being able to count to one hundred at the age of four, I believe the other passengers on the bus would appreciate not having to listen to her continue counting beyond a hundred. Maybe I should just tell her that's it. One hundred is the highest number there is. Nothing comes after it.

"Well, uh, after one hundred, um…"

Ella looks disgusted. "Just admit you don't know, Mommy."

I shake my head. "Maybe you can ask your teacher tomorrow."

"Okay. Mommy, if God made the world, then who made God?"

"Um…yeah, I'm just going to come out and admit that I don't know the answer to that one." I'm tired. I want Ella to stop talking, and I don't want to come up with any more answers.

"But just what do you think, Mommy? Just what do you think? And plus, why is the sky blue and not pink?"

"Because it absorbs all the colors except for blue, and so blue is reflected back into your eyes, and that's what you see. Get it?"

When she doesn't answer, I turn to see that she has fallen asleep, her head slumped back against the seat. The poor little thing must have been exhausted, which is not surprising given that she recently stopped napping. Not to mention the fact that her sleep at night is so poor. I put my arm around her and give her a kiss, leaning her sweet little head onto my shoulder.

As much as it drives me crazy answering all these questions, I know that it's important for Ella to learn all she can about the world. Sometimes Steve and I get in evil moods and joke about horrible things we could do, like teaching Ella her numbers in the wrong order or calling colors different names. Not that we would ever do something like that to her.

A few minutes later, the bus arrives at our stop. On the walk home, Ella sings the alphabet song ten times in a row.

"Next time won't you sing with me!"

"No, El, there is no next time. We are *done* with the alphabet," I say, more harshly than I mean to.

Ella looks hurt. I feel like a terrible mother, but I'm just tired of being "on." Every day I spend almost all day with Ella. She spends a few short hours at Sutterville, but considering the bus ride there and back, I only have a few hours at home, which I use to pick up clutter, blow-dry my hair, and eat lunch. When Steve gets home, we have dinner and spend a little time watching TV, and then I go to bed. On the weekends, I have a bit more leisure time, but it is still spent with Steve and Ella. I can't remember the last time I just relaxed or did anything for myself, other than taking a shower. When was the last time I wrote anything other than a grocery list?

"So write," Becca had said.

Would I be a bad mom if I call a sitter and leave for a few hours? I almost laugh when I realize that I am feeling guilty about the idea of leaving for a few hours, when most moms are only home a few hours a day. As we walk into the house, I decide to do it. I am going to put myself first for the first time in a very long time.

I pick up the phone and dial Maddy's number. Fifteen minutes later, I hear the doorbell ring, and I smile.

"Okay, Maddy, you have my cell phone number. I'm just going to be at Caffé Latte. Just call if you have a problem."

On my way out, on a whim, I grab my old laptop computer out of the closet. Who knows what might happen with a cup of coffee and some free time? At Caffé Latte, I buy an iced mocha and a scone. I turn on my laptop. I feel like I can breathe freely, just having a little space to myself. I take a sip of coffee and look outside at the beautiful spring day. Then I open Word and decide just to free write.

I begin typing. At first, I write something resembling a diary entry about what I've done today, the things I still need to get done, and my frustrations. Then I begin to write about the people around me, describing what they look like and who they might be. But soon, I find that I am writing a story. It is about a woman who has moved to Paris to study art and finds herself falling in love with France and the people there. It is like a beautiful escape, writing about the little fifteenth-century town where she lives. After writing for a while, I look down at the time and am shocked to find that I have been writing for the last three hours. The short story that I had planned to write is clearly a bit more than that. To finish the story I have in my head would take weeks. It would have to be a novel. I sigh, knowing that I couldn't possibly undertake such an endeavor. But somehow, the idea of writing a novel gives me a giddy feeling of excitement that I haven't felt in a long time. Why shouldn't I write a novel? I have a story in my head, and I want to put it down on paper. It would give me a sense of purpose and, even, a sense of fun.

When I get home, I ask Maddy if she could possibly babysit every day for a couple of hours after school.

She grins. "Sure, actually, a steady job sounds good. I'm trying to save up some money right now so that I can buy a used car by the time I get my license."

"Mommy!" Ella says, hugging me around the legs.

I kiss her, and I notice that I no longer feel tired or burned out. In fact, I feel happy that I will be spending the rest of the evening with my little girl.

"I missed you, sweetie," I say as I pick her up. "What do you say we make some stuffed artichokes for dinner?"

Later that evening, long after the dishes have been washed and put away, Steve walks through the door. He puts his briefcase down and gives me a big hug. "What's for dinner, cutie?"

"Stuffed artichokes. Oh, and…guess what?" I say.

"What?"

"I'm writing a novel. About a woman who moves to France and becomes an artist."

Steve kisses me on the top of my head. "That's great. I'm proud of you. But when will you find the time to write?" Steve takes the pan of artichokes out of the refrigerator, removes the plastic wrap on top, and puts an artichoke on a plate.

I smile. "See, that's the best part of the plan." I point to the microwave. "Two minutes should do it. Anyway, you know how tired and stressed I've been lately? Well, I've hired Maddy to come babysit Ella for about three hours every day after school while I write."

"How much are you paying Maddy?" he says.

"Ten bucks an hour."

"That's thirty dollars a day. That's a lot of money, babe."

"It's the going rate," I say.

"Yeah, but that's…what? That's six hundred dollars a month. Does a fifteen-year-old really need that much cash? Why not pay her five an hour?"

"We've been paying her ten, Steve. You know, I would have thought you'd be more supportive. Maybe if you were home more, I would have a chance to write, but you aren't. What do you expect me to do?"

"I don't know," he says. "But we just can't afford that."

"Okay, then, how about an hour a day? We can certainly afford that. I just…I have to do this. I need something besides just being a mom. I'm a writer, and I haven't written anything in three years."

Steve takes his artichoke out of the microwave.

"You're right," he says quietly. "I'm sorry, Angie. I'm just so stressed at work, I can hardly think straight. Of course you should write a novel."

I smile. "That's okay."

"So tell me about the plot."

When we go to bed, Steve spoons me. "I love you so much," he says, kissing my neck.

"I love you too," I say, cuddling against him. "I miss you," I whisper, but he either doesn't hear this or doesn't acknowledge that I've said it.

Friday, April 28, 6:45 p.m.—visit to Sacramento

Steve and I are lying in bed together, Buddy on the foot of the bed. I can hardly believe how wonderful our relationship is turning out to be. It is everything that

I could have hoped for and more. The only problem we have is the knowledge that tomorrow, I have to go back to New York. Steve promised me that he would do everything he could to keep us together, and I know he'll keep his word, but I can't help being afraid.

Steve runs his hand over the curve of my hip. "Angela...what a beautiful name you have."

"I like your name too."

"Eh, Steven, boring," he says. "But Angela is an angel, an angel in an Italian painting."

I lean back against him. I feel so close to him, so accepted by him, just as I do with my husband. But one thing lingers in the back of my brain, eating away at me stealthily from the inside—I have not yet told Steve the truth about my life. I have given him the version that makes me seem sane. And I know that if I am going to be with Steve forever, he is going to have to know. I have been so conflicted, so unsure what to do. But now, lying here in Steve's arms, I feel that it is the right time. He loves me, and if he is anything like the Steve I know, this new information isn't going to change the way he feels about me.

"Steve?" I say, kissing his arm. "What if there was such a thing as an alternate reality? And what if, in an alternate reality, I had grown up in Sacramento and married you?"

Steve nuzzles my neck. "I'd say that would be perfect."

"Yeah...but what if I existed in that reality and then when I went to bed at night, instead of sleeping, I woke up in this reality, the one where I am from New York?"

Steve sits up, always a sucker for science fiction. "Wow. So wait. It would be like every time you go to sleep, you don't sleep, but you actually wake up in your other life?"

Relief floods through me. He's understanding faster than I anticipated. "Yes. Exactly. But I feel refreshed and ready to start a new day."

"That would be a great movie," Steve says.

"Yeah, maybe I could play myself. Or my friend could play me. She's an actress. Well, at least, one version of her was...in one of my lives."

Steve laughs. "Wow, you've really thought this thing through, haven't you?"

I bite my lip, turning to face Steve. "Well, I have, because it's the truth. I know it sounds crazy, and weird, and the alternate-reality version of you had a really hard time understanding at first, but he eventually accepted me for who I am, and I hope that maybe you might be able to as well."

Steve gives me a searching look. "Angie, come on. Be serious. You're kind of weirding me out."

"Steve, I'm being more serious than I've ever been in my life. This really is the truth of my life. And see—my two lives are different but also kind of the same. In my other life, my dad died of cancer. That's how my dad here was able to be cured, because I told him to get tested and the cancer wasn't far enough along yet."

"So, you're what, a fortune-teller?" Steve says.

"No, I'm not. In fact, things are often different. Like, there you're an architect. And sadly, lottery numbers never seem to be the same. Probably because they're random."

Steve pulls away from me. "Seriously? You seriously believe that you inhabit alternate realities?"

"Yes."

"And you believe you're married to an 'alternate version' of me in your other life?"

"Yes. That's how I know you so well. That's why you feel like I've always known you. It's because I've been dating you since I was eighteen. I know things about you that no one else knows. I've cried with you and laughed with you and made a child with you. I know it sounds completely absurd, but it really is the truth." I pull the sheets up around my chin.

Steve thinks for a moment. "Okay, so you say you know me so well. Tell me some things that you know about me."

I purse my lips. "Okay, well, when you were five years old, you wanted to fly like Superman, so you tied a sheet around your neck and jumped out your bedroom window and ended up breaking both of your legs."

Steve massages his temples. "That is creepy that you know that..."

"So I was right?"

"Well, yeah, except I only broke one of my legs."

"And when you were sixteen, you made out with a cheerleader and she gave you mono. It was so bad that you had to quit the swim team."

He shakes his head. "Angie, those are things you could have found out. You could have talked to people who know me. You could have researched."

"But I didn't."

Steve looks pained. I've obviously made a huge mistake. It was way too soon. I keep forgetting that this man is not my husband. To him, this is a new relationship. A relationship that I may have just ruined.

"I'm sorry," he says. "It freaks me out that you found all this stuff out about me, trying to make me think you know me in some alternate universe for I don't know what purpose. It's just weird and crazy."

Weird and crazy. I want to cry, but I can't waste time on tears right now. I have only one chance to convince Steve that this is the truth. I can only hope it doesn't push him further away.

"What if I knew something else?" I say slowly. "What if I knew something that you had never told anyone in your entire life?

"Okay," he says.

I take a deep breath. "Your older cousin, Stan, used to be really mean to you when you were a kid. Every single day he used to make fun of you because you wore glasses. He would get other kids at school to gang up on you. And one day you were so mad that you prayed Stan would get hit by a car. And then, the next day at school, Stan wasn't at recess. And when you got home, your mom was crying and told you that Stan had been hit by a car. He was killed. You were sure that you had done this to him. And you never told anyone—at first because you were afraid you'd be punished, later because you thought no one would believe you, and finally, after you came to accept that it probably had been a coincidence, because the memory was just too painful to revisit. You only told me after we'd been married for a few years."

"Oh my God," Steve says. "I've never told *anybody* about that."

"I know."

Steve backs away from me, looking horrified.

"Please," I say. "I'm not a witch or something." Tears fall down my cheeks.

Steve shrugs, tears filling his eyes too. "I really like you, Angela. But this is just too weird for me. I can't believe what you're saying."

I take his hands in mine. "You don't *have* to," I say. "You just have to believe that I'm telling you what I believe to be true."

Steve squeezes my hands. "I do believe that."

"So then why does it have to end?" I sob. "Why can't you love me despite this?"

Steve puts his head in his hands. "I can love you despite this. I just can't be with you. Even if everything is as you say it is, it's just too weird. How am I supposed to be with a woman who is already married to me and knows all my inner secrets before I'm ready to tell them? I just can't do it. I don't mean to hurt you, Angela. I'm sorry." He kisses the tear on my cheek. "It will be okay. I promise you'll be okay."

I wipe my tears and try to take in what has just happened, but I can't.

"You should go," he says quietly.

I know that when I walk out the door, I'm never going to see him again. Why, oh why was I so stupid? I could have waited years to tell him.

That night in my bed at the hotel, I cry until I wake up next to my husband.

Chapter 41

Saturday, April 29, 8:01 a.m., Sacramento

I NUZZLE INTO my spot under Steve's arm, tears still running down my cheeks.

Steve stirs. He reaches down with his hand and brushes the skin under my eyes. "You're crying. What's the matter?"

"You dumped me," I say, sobbing.

Steve sits up in bed groggily. "I did what?"

"You dumped me. I told you about my two lives, and you couldn't take it. At first you didn't believe me, and you thought I was a crazy stalker, but then I told you about Stan, and I think it just freaked you out. And you said you still love me but you can't be with me because it's too much for you to handle. You told me to leave."

"Oh, honey…" Steve cuddles me close to him and kisses away my tears. "I'm so sorry, baby. I guess I'm a jerk over there, huh? Well, I'm not worth it then."

"No, Steve," I say. "The problem is that you aren't a jerk. You're perfect. It was just too soon, I guess. And now I've ruined it."

Steve sighs. "I think you should just leave and go back to New York. You've still got me, remember? I'm not going anywhere. Come on. Let's go have some breakfast."

Steve makes scrambled eggs, and he even gives me cocoa with cinnamon and almond extract. My favorite breakfast. It tastes good, and I enjoy eating next to Steve and Ella, my little family.

It is amazing how comforting a little child can be. Later, we take Ella to Funderland, and she rides the spinning cups, the tiny roller coaster with baby hills, the helicopters, and the bumper cars.

We have a nice day together, but I can't help being consumed with worry about what is happening with the other Steve.

Saturday, April 29, 8:02 a.m.—visit to Sacramento

I wake up in my bed at the Hyatt. Every day of this visit before today, I have woken up feeling so hopeful and happy. Now I feel deflated and apprehensive. My heart beating rapidly, I pick up my cell phone and call Steve.

"Hello?" Steve sounds groggy, as though he has just woken up. I can hear Buddy barking in the background.

"Hi, it's Angie," I say.

"Hi."

My heart is brimming over with all the things I want to say to him. I want to tell him how hurt and disappointed I am that he wasn't able to be there for me. I want to tell him I love him. So I take a deep breath, open my mouth…and lie.

"Steve, I'm sorry about last night. I just sometimes let my imagination run away with me? I probably am just a narcoleptic with a very interesting dream life."

Steve sighs. "That's very possible. And that wouldn't bother me. It's just, all that stuff you knew about me…I just…Angie, I'm sorry, but I meant what I said last night."

"Steve, I know you love me," I say. "Do you really want to lose me forever?"

"No, I really don't, Angie," he says quietly, hanging up the phone. And I am left wondering whether he meant that he really doesn't love me or that he really doesn't want to lose me.

I take out my laptop and begin writing an email.

Dear Steve,

I have so much I'd like to say to you, and I wish that we could speak in person, but I know you don't want to right now. I am sorry that I lied to you. I didn't lie to you last night, but I did lie to you this morning, on the phone. I am not a person with an overactive imagination, and I am not crazy. I am a normal person just trying to live a normal life like everyone else I know. My life has been very painful as a result of this situation I am in, although it has also been very rich. I have had twice as many birthday parties as everyone I know, twice as many first kisses...but I have also had twice as many embarrassing and upsetting moments.

I don't know why I live in two alternate realities. Maybe everyone does and I'm the only one who retains the memory of my other life. Maybe there are others out there like me, although I have yet to meet one. For me, each life is as real as the other. And there have been occurrences that seem impossible if one life was only a dream. My dad's illness was one. And all the things I knew about your past...

And yes, I suppose that does come across as creepy, but remember that although I am a stranger to you, you are my husband in my other life. We have a daughter together, a beautiful little girl named Ella, and you love her with all of your heart. I will never forget you.

Angela

I hit send, tears running down my cheeks. Then I hurriedly pack my bags and check out of the hotel. It is time for me to go home. I have no other choice.

As I board the plane, a tear runs down my cheek.

"I know just how you feel, sweetheart," a flight attendant says, patting me on the shoulder.

No, no you don't.

Thankfully, the flight is not full, and I am able to secure a row of seats to myself. I sit by the window and look out, thinking about what I've lost, and crying. Later, the flight attendants come by with a cart of snacks, but I am unable to eat. I feel like I'll never be able to eat again. My eyes are swollen from crying, and I just feel exhausted. At one point, we hit a turbulent patch, and I am forced to throw up in the little paper bag the airline provides.

When I arrive back at my apartment, I see that my tenant has left things in good condition. On the table, I find a note on pink stationary. *Thanks for letting me stay here. I enjoyed reading your plays. Some guy named Tony kept calling. You should probably call him back. Anyway, thanks again!*

I check my voicemail. Fifty-three messages. Amid the calls from telemarketers are several messages from Tony.

"Hi, Ang, it's Tony." His voice sounds very fake and sickly sweet. "Listen—I think yesterday was a serious misunderstanding. I would never have forced you to do anything you didn't want to do. I understand that you were just having a bad dream and that you overreacted. And in light of that, I forgive you for punching me. Okay, honey? Call me. Love you."

"Hi, Angie, baby, I would appreciate a call back. Come on. I know you're there. Pick up the phone."

"Hi, Angie, please pick up." Tony's voice sounds desperate now, and he is clearly drunk. "Your cell phone message box is full. I can't reach you. Come on. Pick up! I love you. Angie, I need you."

Rapidly, the messages grow bitter.

"Please…pick up the fucking phone…You bitch! You fucking bitch!" I can hear him crying over the phone. "You are mine. You belong to me. If you can't understand that, then fuck you! It's over. We're over!"

"Hello, Angie, um, this is Tony. I'm sorry for my message last night. I was drunk. I would appreciate at least a phone call."

"Hello, Angela. I went to your parents' house, and they said you moved to California, but I know they're lying. Obviously you are here and screening your calls."

"Hello, Angela, I'd just like to tell you that I have a new girlfriend. And she isn't frigid. I hope you enjoy your new life in 'California.'"

I delete all the messages and fall into bed, exhausted. I don't even want to think about Tony right now. His words make me feel no emotions, no anger, no sadness, just…nothing. I simply don't care.

Chapter 42

Thursday, May 4, 3:43 p.m., New York

SINCE SATURDAY, I have stayed in my apartment, crying until I throw up. In all the years of my life, through breakups, depressions, even the death of my father, I have never had emotional pain cause me to become so physically ill. In only these few days, I have lost five pounds because I haven't been able to eat—and the little I have eaten, I've thrown up. I lie in the middle of my bed in the fetal position, crying and crying. My nose is snotty, and my eyes are red. I haven't even showered today. All of a sudden, I run to the bathroom just in time to throw up for the fifth time today. I lean back against the cool wall of the bathroom and close my eyes. I can't remember the last time I threw up this much. Even when I have the flu, I usually manage to only throw up once or twice. The last time I was this sick was when I was pregnant with Ella.

Oh God.

On the floor of my bathroom, I frantically calculate how long it's been since my last period, and I realize, with a sense of horror, that it is definitely late. I was so excited to be with Steve in California that I didn't even notice my period hadn't come. I can't believe this is happening to me. My head is swimming.

I rinse out my mouth with mouthwash, throw on a pair of jeans and an old T-shirt, and walk to Duane Reade, where I buy three different brands of pregnancy tests. Thirty minutes later, I am confirmed pregnant by all three.

I survey the situation. *I just got pregnant by the alternate reality version of my husband.* More than anything, I want to call him. To tell him that I'm carrying his baby. But I can't. Knowing Steve, if he knew I was pregnant, he would take me back. But it wouldn't be the same. I would always know that he was only with me because he felt it was his duty.

I guess I am going to be a single mom. And somehow, the thought doesn't terrify me the way that it probably should. I can't help but feel happy knowing that Steve's child is growing inside me. Maybe now I'll have another little version of Ella to keep me company and be my little sidekick. I just wish I could have Steve too.

The phone rings. "Hi, Angela," Jana says. "How was California?"

In response, I burst into tears.

"Oh, no, sweetie, is this about Tony? Did he do something to you?"

"No," I say. "It's not him. I met someone in California. But it didn't work out. And I'm pregnant."

"Oh. My. God." Jana sighs deeply. "Do your parents know about this?"

"Not yet," I say.

"What are you going to do?"

"I want it!" I say, more passionately than I intended.

"You want it?" she says incredulously.

"Yeah, I love Steve, and I want his baby."

"Does this 'Steve' know you're pregnant?"

"No," I say. "And I'm not telling him, because I don't want him to be with me out of obligation."

"Oh, honey bunny. This is just crazy…Look, whatever you choose to do, I support you. I do—you know that. I just…I'm kind of in shock now. But listen. I'll call you tomorrow and see how you're doing, okay?"

I grab my bag and head over to my parents' apartment.

"So this guy is just leaving you to raise his kid alone?" my mom says, on the verge of tears. "I thought you said he is your husband out in California. Isn't he supposed to love you?"

I start to tear up as well. "Yeah, Mom, he is. But apparently he doesn't in this life."

My dad, of course, threatens to "kill him." I tell him that killing the father of my child surprisingly won't make me feel any better.

As much as my parents are unhappy, however, a certain excitement wins out when they realize that they are going to be having their first grandchild.

"Oh, Angie, maybe we can go shopping for some pretty maternity clothes," my mother says.

"Sure, Mom. But I don't think it's necessary yet. To tell you the truth, I've been puking so much that I've lost five pounds."

At this, my mom becomes concerned and spends the rest of the conversation reading me passages from an old, battered copy of *What to Expect When You're Expecting*, despite my continual reassurances that I have actually been through all of this before and know exactly what to expect already. I assure her that yes, I know I need to take folic acid and vitamins, and no, I'm not drinking or smoking. And yes, I know not to change cat litter, which should be especially easy to avoid since I don't have a cat and am not in the habit of changing other people's cat-litter boxes.

When I get home, I am thoroughly exhausted. I end up making myself some cream of wheat and watching *Mary Poppins*. If only Mary Poppins could come fix all my problems with a song and a trip to a happy cartoon world.

Monday, May 8, 5:28 p.m., Sacramento

"Ella, you need to take four more bites before you go play," I say.

Ella has only eaten two bites of her dinner, and I know that she is holding out for a piece of cake that is in the refrigerator.

"No," she says.

"Four more bites," I say again. I wish that Steve was home. I miss him, especially because I'm missing him so much in New York. If I could only come back here to find him waiting happily for me, it might help me get past my heartbreak. Unfortunately, he has been working more than ever. I know that his firm is putting a lot of pressure on him, even though he doesn't seem to want to talk about it. Still, all the telltale signs are there. He has been putting in lots of overtime and coming home late every night.

After Ella finishes her four bites, she runs up to her room to play, and I give Steve a call on his cell phone. He doesn't answer, so I call him on his work phone.

"Steve? When are you coming home?"

"Not for a while, Ang," he says, his voice sounding tired. "I've still got a lot of work to do."

"I know, but couldn't you work at home?"

"Not on this. I probably won't be home until late. Don't wait up."

"No, Steve," I say. "That sucks. I'm tired of you not getting home until after I'm asleep. I need you, and our daughter needs you."

"Yeah, well, work needs me too. I'm trying to support you guys."

"Well, that's wonderful, but I think you could still support us without working every moment of your life. You aren't even enjoying work anymore. You need to get your priorities straight. I just feel like I am the last thing on your list. After you work and spend time with Ella and sleep and eat and watch TV, then maybe you might have two seconds to get to me. I feel like I'm losing you in both of my lives."

Steve sighs. "Angela, I don't have time to have this conversation right now. I've got a lot of work to do."

"Great," I say. "It's really wonderful that you don't even have the time to discuss the fact that you have no time for me."

"Well, right now I don't."

"Fine. Just don't expect me to be there for you next time you need me."

I hang up on him. Hot tears sting my eyes. I want my husband back.

I hear Ella's feet come padding down the stairs.

"Is Daddy coming home?" she says hopefully.

I feel so bad, that I let her eat a piece of chocolate cake in front of the TV.

Chapter 43

Tuesday, May 9, 7:00 p.m., Sacramento

I KNOW THAT Steve came home last night, because there are a few dirty dishes in the sink. He never came to bed though. He must have slept on the couch.

I haven't called him all day, because I haven't wanted to fight with him, but the truth is that I have thought about little else other than him all day. The only relief I had was when I was writing. Then, I was able to submerge myself in another world, where I am the one who decides what happens.

My mom comes over for dinner, and I tell her about what is going on in my marriage.

"Oh, sweetie," she says. "Just after you solved one problem, here you two go with another."

"Do you think he's punishing me, Mom? Do you think this is his way of getting back at me for what happened with Tony?"

She takes a bite of lasagna and shakes her head. "No, honey, I think his long hours were his way of punishing you before, but I don't think that's what's going on now. He seems unhappy and distracted. But he doesn't seem angry with you."

I had to agree with her. "It's true. Things are fine between us when he's here, except that he is stressed out. The problem is just that he is hardly ever here anymore."

"I know. And it isn't fair to Ella or you. He needs to understand that he is going to miss his life. He's going to miss these precious times with his daughter. Before you know it, Ella's a teenager, and then she's out of the house. Have you talked to him?"

"Um, yeah, we've talked, all right. He just doesn't seem willing to do anything to change the situation. So I don't really know what to do."

"Life is so short," she says. "And in the end, he'll never regret not working enough. But he will regret not spending enough time with his family."

After my mom leaves, I have an overwhelming urge to talk to Steve. I hadn't planned on calling tonight, but I just want to hear his voice. I dial his cell phone, and again, he has it turned off. When I call work, the administrative assistant answers.

"Hi, Cynthia," I say. "Is Steve there?"

I hear hesitation in her voice. "He isn't with you?"

"No, did he leave already?"

"Well…yes," she says. "He actually left several hours ago, and he said he was going home, but maybe he decided to go somewhere else. Have you, uh…have you talked to him today?"

"No." Now I am suspicious. Something is definitely going on here, and I don't like it.

"Oh, well, look. I don't know why he hasn't told you, but he actually left the job this morning. I'm not sure what happened. I don't really know if he quit or was let go."

"What?"

I can't believe what I'm hearing. If he quit, part of me feels thrilled that Steve paid attention to what I've been telling him. But a larger part of me is furious. I know that Steve didn't get any other job offers. I don't know how easy he thinks it will be to get a new job, but I do know that the responsible thing would have been to find a new job before quitting his current one.

"I'm surprised he hasn't called you."

"Me too. Thanks, Cynthia." I hang up and massage my temples.

Two hours later, I am really worried. If Steve quit this morning, where the hell has he been all day, and why hasn't he called me? I don't think that he would ever do anything to deliberately hurt himself, but it just isn't like Steve to act this erratically.

By eleven o'clock, I am calling hospitals in the area. No one matching Steve's description has been admitted. At midnight, I call the cops, but they tell me they can do nothing until someone has been missing for forty-eight hours. I leave several messages on Steve's voice mail, but he doesn't call back. Finally, at twelve thirty I collapse onto my bed, awakened in New York by the sound of my phone ringing.

Tuesday, May 9, 3:30 p.m., New York

"Hi, hon, it's Jana. I was wondering if you wanted to go see a movie tonight."

"I don't know," I say. "Maybe tomorrow. I'm just really upset about Steve."

What she doesn't know is that I'm really upset about both of my Steves.

"Come on," she says. "You need to get out of the house. Please come out."

"Okay," I say. I have to acknowledge to myself that whether I mope around or not, Steve isn't coming back to me.

I meet Jana at Union Square around seven o'clock. She looks so pretty in a pair of knee-high boots and a red skirt. I feel like a total slob next to her in an old T-shirt and a ratty pair of denim shorts, my eyes still swollen from too much crying.

"Angie!" Jana says, running to me and giving me a huge hug. "Oh, honey. What on earth have you been doing? You are a total mess."

I nod, embarrassed.

Jana takes my arm. "Okay, here is what we are going to do. We're going to see this movie, and then tomorrow I'm taking you to a day spa, and you are getting a manicure and pedicure and a facial. Just because you feel like shit doesn't mean you have to look like it. Besides, you are going to have a baby. You want to bring it into this world with a stable mom, right?"

I nod, grateful that Jana is going to take care of me, since I seem unable to care for myself.

Chapter 44

Wednesday, May 10, 8:04 a.m., Sacramento

When I wake up, Steve is not beside me. I am gripped with a terrible panic. Rushing out of bed, my clothes still on from last night, I run downstairs. There is no sign that Steve has been here...He didn't come home last night. Terrible visions start racing through my brain, a picture of Steve drowned in the Sacramento River, a picture of Steve's car wrecked on the freeway, a picture of Steve driving his car into the distance, leaving me forever. I call his cell phone. No answer. Then I begin to cry. *Steve, where are you?*

The door opens, and I turn around. Steve is standing in the doorway. I simultaneously want to punch him in the face and kiss him for an hour. I do neither.

"Where have you been?" I say, my voice quivering.

"I'm sorry, Angie. I'm so sorry." Steve's eyes fill with tears. "I fell asleep in the car."

"What?"

He takes a deep breath. "Yesterday, I talked to John and told him that I needed more time for my family and that I wanted to cut back on work. He was a total asshole, and we got into it. And he ended up firing me. I thought you'd be mad, so I was avoiding coming home. That's why my phone was off."

"Where did you go?" I whisper.

"Angie, I'm an idiot. I went to a bar, and I got kind of tipsy. And then I knew I couldn't drive, so I went and had dinner, and I sat in the park for a couple of hours. But then, when I was driving home, I was falling asleep at the wheel, so I pulled over to the side of the road to take a little nap and...I actually just woke up about ten minutes ago."

"Do you know how worried I was?" I say, raising my voice. "I thought you were dead." Tears roll down my cheeks. "I thought something happened to you!"

Steve takes me in his arms. "I'm sorry, baby. I was stupid. I want to be here for you and Ella. I'm going to find a different job, and everything is going to be good again. I promise."

Steve kisses me, and for the first time in a long time, I feel like everything is going to be okay.

Saturday, September 2, 3:00 p.m., New York

In the months since I have found out that I was pregnant, things have progressed surprisingly well, except, of course, for the fact that the father of my baby is not here. He doesn't even know he is going to be a father. Every single day is a constant battle with myself not to call him. The morning sickness I was having is mostly gone now, but the grieving for Steve remains.

I stand in front of the mirror, brushing my hair, and I turn to the side, looking at my belly. I can clearly see the bulge in my stomach underneath my black tank top. I am showing enough, anyway, that the director of *Glengarry Glen Ross* at the Atlantic asked me when I was due.

I tuck a strand of hair behind my ear. I have the look of a happy pregnant woman: the glow, the tightly stretched belly. I just don't have the man. I sigh and put on some lipstick and then slip on some black flats and grab my bag. I hesitate before leaving my apartment, glancing at the phone, willing it to ring. Then I take a deep breath and leave, locking the dead bolt behind me. I walk the two blocks to Whole Foods quickly. I am desperately craving its bite-sized brownies.

In the produce section of Whole Foods, I buy a bag of bananas, which I will use mainly as a vehicle for peanut butter. As I turn to put the bag in my cart, I see someone familiar out of the corner of my eye. I turn to say hello…and I realize that it is Tony. I turn my head away, praying that he didn't see me. I'll never understand how, in a city the size of New York, I can't seem to go anywhere without running into someone I know. Quickly, I wheel my cart around the oranges. He doesn't see me, but I now have a good view of him. I notice that his nose looks a little out of joint, as if it has healed badly. He is with a woman. She is very pretty, very petite, almost impossibly skinny. The woman's blond hair is pulled back into a ponytail, and she is giggling as Tony rubs his hand down her butt.

Suddenly, my morning sickness is back, and I have an urge to throw up all over the floor. Instead, I swallow hard and breathe deeply. I want to run to that woman and tell her to stay far, far away from Tony. I'd like to tell her that he doesn't know how to take no for an answer. But I can't stomach the thought of Tony even seeing me. I push my cart out of the produce aisle and take off toward the pasta aisle.

My heart beating rapidly, I grab a box of whole wheat pasta and a can of Newman's Own tomato sauce and decide that the bite-sized brownies can wait. I just need to get out of this store. I begin walking quicker, desperate to get out. I wheel around the corner, and bam! I run right into someone else's cart. That someone is Tony and his new girlfriend.

Tony stares at me. I grasp for words, a fake smile coming to my lips, unbidden.

"Hi, Angela," he says, coldly. "This is my girlfriend, Crystal. Crystal, Angela, my ex."

Crystal gives me a big, fake smile. "Hi, nice to meet you," she says, holding out her hand.

I step out from behind my cart and shake it stiffly. "Nice to meet you too," I say, as if by rote.

"Ooh," Crystal says, putting her hand on my belly.

I shudder.

"When are you due?" she says.

I look at Tony, and I see panic in his eyes. I suddenly realize that he must think it's his. "January," I say, a smile playing on the edges of my lips.

Tony tenses up. "So, uh, are you, um, seeing anyone right now?" he says.

"No, I'm not."

His eyes grow wide with fear, and Crystal's face twists from cooing excitement to perplexity.

"Wait a minute," she says, pointing at Tony. "Is that yours?"

"No!" Tony says. Then he looks at me. "It isn't mine...is it?"

"No," I say. "Thank goodness...How's your nose, by the way?"

Crystal looks confused.

Tony gives me a dirty look. The morning sickness overtakes me, and before I have a chance to even turn around, I throw up all over Tony's Italian leather shoes. Amid a torrent of swear words, I turn my cart around and run in the opposite direction, hoping I never run into Tony again.

When I get home, I put my groceries away and rush over to the YMCA on Fourteenth, where I am taking a class in the Bradley Method of childbirth. Jana has graciously agreed to stand in for Steve during the labor. Today is the first meeting of the weekly class. I meet Jana outside of the YMCA.

"Hi."

Jana gives me a big hug. "You look good. You have that cute little bump now." She pats my stomach, "Hey there, little one."

"Guess who I ran into?" I say.

"Not Tony?"

I raise my eyebrow. "Good guess. He had a new girlfriend. Crystal. She looked about ten years old." I laugh. "He thought the baby was his at first."

"I love it! What an ass!"

"Yeah. I actually feel sorry for the girlfriend. Jana, she couldn't have been more than eighteen years old. I'm serious. She probably goes to NYU. I hope she dumps his ass."

"What a piece of work. So was his nose broken, after all?"

I smile. "It looked kind of bent out of shape...And I threw up on his shoes."

"You threw up on his shoes?"

I start to laugh. "Yeah."

Jana puts her arm around me. "Well, good, he deserved it."

Still giggling, we walk down the dingy hallway and into a room with a photocopied sign on the door, which read Bradley Class, 5:00.

Inside the room are six couples sitting in a circle on the floor.

"Come on in, ladies." The woman speaking looks to be in her early forties, with a head of bright-red curly hair and black velour sweatpants.

Jana and I grab two chairs and join the circle. We listen to the woman, who introduces herself as Lena, as she explains the philosophy behind the Bradley method. We are doing this method, she says, so that we can have a natural, drug-free birthing process that is as free from pain as possible. Another benefit is that we will be coached by our husbands.

She turns to me and Jana and says, "Or in your case, by your birth partner."

Lena goes on to give us a list of the things we should and should not be eating while we are pregnant. The "should" list includes protein items, dairy products, and fresh fruits and vegetables. Conspicuously absent are bite-sized brownies and peanut butter.

I raise my hand. "This is just a guideline, right? When we have cravings, we can have stuff like brownies and peanut butter, right?"

A woman with long, black hair pulled back by a headband, a yoga mat sticking out of her bag, and a husband who looks like a Calvin Klein model, shoots me a horrified look.

"Just as examples," I say.

Lena shakes her head, swinging her large silver hoop earrings. "Occasionally, but if you want brownies, try having some fresh fruit instead. Husbands, you should try to keep the house well stocked with healthy food and encourage your wife by eating healthy along with her and helping keep track of what she's eating. After all, it's your baby too."

Jana raises her hand. "So I'm supposed to come between a pregnant woman and her bite-sized brownies?"

"Well, the best way to be loving and supportive of your partner during this time is to help her stay healthy so that she stays low risk and so that she can bring your baby into the world in a natural way."

After talking about prenatal vitamins and the importance of exercise during pregnancy, Lena announces that we are going to end the class with the husbands massaging the wives. We are told that it would be a nice way to end each day, for the wife to be given a massage before bed. I feel a pang of sadness, wishing that I had Steve here beside me during my pregnancy. Instead, I have Jana, who, while here for me, isn't quite the same as a husband. After class, Jana and I go to Starbucks, where I break the diet rules in record time, buying a big maple nut scone and a decaf coffee.

"Thanks, Jana," I say. "I couldn't do this without you."

Friday, September 8, 6:30 p.m., Sacramento

"Well, can't he just get a job at the Home Depot or something? Just in the meantime?"

I am sitting with Becca at Florez Grill, having a girls' night. Steve is watching our kids. I take a sip of the giant watermelon margarita we are sharing.

"If he has to," I say. "But we're hoping he finds something soon."

Becca dips a tortilla chip in salsa. "Yeah, every little bit helps, right? How are you guys paying your mortgage?"

I raise my eyebrow. "We're using our savings and some inheritance money, which is supposed to pay for Ella to go to college. Supposedly, we'll pay back the account when Steve gets a new job, but that seems to be taking a little longer than planned."

"Well, is he looking?"

I take another sip of margarita, already feeling a little bit giddy. "That's the thing," I say. "I mean, he *is*. He's looking at job listings and stuff, but he isn't really proactively looking. I can tell he's kind of depressed about the whole being-out-of-work thing, and honestly, I think he feels stupid for getting in that argument with his boss. And there just aren't a lot of jobs open in his field right now. Plus, I'm not willing to move."

"But he did this for you, right?" Becca says.

"He did. And I feel awful. I wish I hadn't pushed him so hard, you know?"

"Sure. Well, are you guys getting along better now?"

I smile. "Yeah, it's nice just to have him home. He is spending lots of time with Ella, and he watches her while I work on my novel. He's actually taken a lot of interest in my writing, which is nice. I like to be able to share it with him. Unfortunately, the kid still isn't sleeping through the night most of the time. You'd think by age four...But she has these night terrors. Thank goodness Steve deals with that."

"Really? That's good of him. Jayden has bad dreams sometimes too. But it's always me that has to deal. Be thankful you've got a husband, even if he is unemployed. Oh, but speaking of men...I have a date tomorrow. Guess who."

"Um, I have no clue," I say.

She smiles guiltily. "Okay, but guess where I met him."

"On the Internet."

"Nope."

"Where then?"

"At Sutterville. I'm going out with Aiden M.'s dad. Isn't that funny? I'm totally, like, trolling my son's preschool for guys. He seems nice. He's been divorced for two years, and he is obviously pretty involved, since he helps out at the preschool. He said his wife left him for some guy she met at the gym."

I smile and stir the margarita with my straw. "Sounds good. Wait, is Aiden M. the kid who picks his nose and eats it?"

Becca laughs. "No, that's Aiden N. Aiden M. is the kid who wears that cute little pilot's jacket every day."

"Oh, his dad is hot!"

Becca nods. "I just hope it works out. Things could get awkward if I have to see him the next day at preschool."

When I get home, Ella is upstairs in bed, and Steve has passed out in front of the TV. I climb onto Steve's lap and kiss him. He opens his eyes groggily.

"Hey, cutie," he says. Then he wrinkles his nose. "Whoa, someone had some tequila."

I laugh.

"You know, I put Ella to bed," he whispers.

"I know," I whisper back, unbuttoning his shirt.

Later, as we are going to sleep, I rest my head on Steve's chest. "I wish I could take you with me to New York. I want you to be there for me through this pregnancy."

He strokes my hair. "I know. I wish I could be there. Honey…I really think you should tell me, or tell *him*, that you're pregnant. He deserves to know. If I know myself at all, he'll be there for you."

My eyes fill with tears. "I know you think that. Anyway, it's okay," I say, trying to convince myself that it is. "I have you here, and that's enough."

Chapter 45

Friday, September 8, 11:04 a.m., New York

I WAKE UP alone in my bed, and I feel like I'm drowning.

I drag myself up and splash water on my face. Whenever I have a particularly wonderful time with Steve in California, it only makes it that much harder to spend the next day without him. Every fiber of my being aches for Steve. I go back to my bed and curl up against my pillow, imagining how it would be if he was here. He would cradle me and put his ear to my stomach, and he would tell our baby how happy he was that it was coming. I close my eyes and try to conjure him up beside me. I can almost smell him. I clutch the pillow tighter and imagine that his arm is around me. *Steve.*

"Steve..." I say out loud. "Steve!"

I start to cry, releasing tears I have held in for the last few months, ever since the initial breakup. It is really hitting me now that I can't have him, that he won't be here for me as I give birth, that he'll never see his child, that he might even marry someone else. I sob until I run out of tears.

Rubbing my stomach, I whisper, "It's okay, little baby. Lots of kids don't have a daddy. You won't be alone."

And for the first time, it hits me, really truly hits me. I have a little person inside of me. Not just my baby, but a person who is going to deserve a daddy.

"I'm sorry, baby," I say. "I'm sorry Mommy was selfish."

In that moment, I decide that no matter what the consequences, Steve deserves to know that I'm having his baby. It has nothing to do with me. It has to do with his baby. If Steve is anything, he is a good father.

I pick up the phone, my heart beating rapidly. I am terrified of talking to Steve. I can't just blurt out that I'm having a baby, can I? The phone rings four times, and then voice mail turns on.

"Hi, it's Steve. Leave a message." His warm, kind voice reaches me across the line, and a lump the size of a softball grows in my throat.

I know I should call back and talk to him in person; it isn't fair to leave a message like this. But part of me is so relieved that I can talk to voice mail and not to him. Words start spilling from my mouth before I can stop them.

"Steve, hi, it's Angela. I know that I am horrible to leave you a message like this, but I won't be a selfish mom, so you have to know: I'm going to have your baby. I know I should have told you before. But you do have a right to know and to be the dad. So I'm telling you. And...I love you." My voice breaks, and I hang up the phone.

"I tried, baby," I say, rubbing my belly.

Saturday, September 9, 6:00 p.m., New York

Steve hasn't returned my call. I keep trying to rationalize it. Maybe he is scared and simply doesn't know what to say to me. The truth though, I have to admit to myself, is that he simply doesn't care. He has written me out of his life. How else can I explain the fact that he hasn't tried to contact me all summer? Not a text, not a phone call, nothing. I haven't contacted him either, but he knew that I would be with him if I could. He is the one who has rejected me. And now, even knowing that I am carrying his child, he hasn't called me back. Not even a call just to say he got the message and that he'll send child support. Nothing.

I think about eating dinner, but the idea of food makes me queasy right now. Instead, I lie down on the bed, listening to Fiona Apple, staring at the ceiling, silently begging Steve to call. I pick up the phone, dial his number, and hang up before the phone rings. Five minutes later, I dial again. This time I wait until I hear his message before I hang up. Maybe after my message yesterday, Steve is screening his calls. Finally, I decide to leave another message.

"Steve, please call me back. I don't need anything from you, I just want to talk—that's it. I just—"

I hear someone pounding on my door, and I hang up midsentence and go to the door.

I open it, and there in jeans and a baseball cap, holding a bouquet of yellow roses, is Steve. I look at him, and I just start to shake. He takes one look at my pregnant belly, and I know that he didn't know. He must not have listened to my message. He always was terrible at checking his voicemail. Steve steadies me and leads me to the couch, one hand on my elbow, the other on my back.

"What are you doing here?" I say. I can hardly comprehend that he is here, in my New York apartment, sitting on my couch.

Steve puts his hand on my chin and tilts my face up to his. "Angie, I'm so sorry. I was just scared."

"You think I'm crazy. You don't believe me, and you think I'm a nutso stalker."

"You've been crying," he says, brushing my lashes with his fingers.

"Well…hormones." I nod.

He smiles and touches my stomach. "You're pregnant."

"I'm having your baby. I'm sorry I didn't tell you sooner, I left a message on your cell phone last night. I didn't want you to feel obligated, if you didn't want me." My voice breaks, and I see Steve's eyes fill with tears.

"Ang, I had this whole speech planned out, but I forgot what I was going to say. The thing is just this: I love you more than I've ever loved anyone in my life, and I want to be with you…It took me a long time to admit it to myself, but the truth is that I can't live without you. I haven't stopped thinking about you for a second since you left. I picked up the phone to call you so many times, but then I just disconnected. And here you were, sitting pregnant and alone. The stuff you knew about me…there is only one way you could have known that, and it just freaked me out. But the more I think about it, the more I know. And I believe you."

Tears run down my cheeks, even as I'm smiling. "This is like a dream," I say. "I just can't believe you're here."

Steve holds me in his arms and kisses me deeply, holding me so tightly I can hardly breathe.

"What happens now?" I say.

"We're together," he says.

"So…what, long distance and all that?"

Steve stares out the window, thinking, and then in one move he is kneeling on the floor and holding my hand. "Marry me."

I look at him in disbelief. "Steve, please, don't do this just because of the baby. This isn't 1950."

He shakes his head. "No, Angela, I'm surer about this than I have ever been about anything…You just have to marry me, because otherwise I don't know what I'll do."

"Yes," I say. "Yes, Steve, of course I'll marry you. But how is this going to work?"

"We'll make it work. I'll move here. I can find work as a musician in the city. We'll have a baby, and we'll make a family." His eyes scan my apartment. "Although, I think we'll have to get a bigger place."

Chapter 46

Wednesday, September 13, 4:00 p.m., Sacramento

Ella and I are in the kitchen, making peanut butter balls with honey and dried milk, when Steve walks downstairs, dressed in a suit and tie and carrying a briefcase.

"Where are you going, honey?" I say.

"Job interview," he says, walking out the door.

I look at Ella, shocked, and then pop a peanut butter ball into my mouth.

"What's a job interview?" Ella says.

"Something that makes Mommy very happy."

Two hours later, Steve returns with a big smile on his face.

"I think I just got a job," he says.

"Where? I didn't even know you had an interview."

"I didn't want to say anything yet, until I knew, but my friend Mike works for this firm, and he put in a good word for me. I didn't want to get your hopes up. But Mike said that the atmosphere there is pretty laid back and they don't expect much overtime. I don't know for sure that I got hired, but they sent me home with forms to fill out for health care and stuff.

"Ahh!" I scream. "Okay, you *so* just got hired. We have to celebrate."

Steve smiles and takes a bottle of wine from the cabinet.

"That stuff is expensive," I say.

"Yeah, well, this is a special occasion."

And then we drink wine and eat peanut butter balls, and that night, Steve seems happier than I have seen him in months.

"I love you so much, my beautiful bride," he whispers, holding me close.

"I love you too." And everything, at least in this life, is perfect once again.

Saturday, September 16, 8:00 p.m., New York

Steve and I arrive at my parents' apartment, giggling as we walk up the stairs together. I haven't told anyone that Steve and I are back together, much less that we are getting married. I thought that my baby shower would be the perfect time to do it.

Over the course of the week, Steve and I have hardly left my apartment, kissing, watching movies, and drinking chocolate milkshakes, my new obsession. We only went out to go to my Bradley class. I called Jana and told her I was sick and wouldn't be able to make it. When I showed up with Steve, Lena looked shocked.

"Is this the father?" she said.

"Yes."

"And so who will be coaching you, Jana or the father?"

"I will be," Steve said, squeezing my hand.

Now, we knock on the door of my parents' apartment, fashionably late. My mom answers the door.

"Mom," I say, the smile on my face so big I fear it will leave permanent marks, "this is Steve. He is moving to New York. And we're getting married."

My mother, bless her heart, lets out a blood-curdling scream. "Ah!"

The party stops. Everyone—my dad, my brother, my aunts and uncles, Jana, and all my other friends—turn and look to the door.

"The baby's father is here!" my mom says. "And Angela's getting married!"

From there, the party passes in a whirlwind. I am showered with advice and birth stories as well as gifts. Everyone congratulates Steve and seems to like him.

As the party is winding down, I find my dad and Steve in a corner, talking about basketball. My dad pats Steve on the back.

"This is a good guy you've got here, Angie. A good guy." I smile, returning to the kitchen to help my mom clean up.

"What do you think of Steve?" I say. "Dad seems to be hitting it off with him."

"Oh, Angie," she says, her eyes filling with tears yet again. "All I ever wanted was for you to be happy. And I can just tell you will be happy with Steve. I can see that he really loves you."

I hug her. "Thanks, Mom."

Monday, September 18, 12:21 p.m., New York

The technician glides the ultrasound wand along my belly. I clutch Steve's hand and look down at the beautiful princess-cut diamond ring on my left hand, the engagement ring Steve bought for me the day after he proposed spontaneously. We picked up our marriage license the same day.

The ceremony is set for next week. Steve's family is going to fly out from California. Jana begged me to wait until after the baby was born so I wouldn't be a pregnant bride, but I decided that I didn't care. I've already had the fairy-tale wedding, just out of college. This time, all I care about is being married to the man I love.

"Do you want to know the sex of the child?" the technician says.

I bite my lip and look up at Steve. He nods. I know that both of us are wondering: Will the baby be Ella? I've told him so much about her that he almost feels like she is his child, which, in a way, she is.

"Well," the technician says happily, "you're going to have a little girl!"

A girl. I'm going to have a girl. *Ella.* But then I realize, stupidly, that of course it couldn't be Ella. But that's okay. I am filled with joy that I am going to have another girl.

And suddenly the realization hits me that now it is more important than ever that both of my lives are real. Because in each life I will have a different child, each as precious to me as the other.

Chapter 47

Wednesday, January 10, 12:01 p.m., Sacramento

I AM HOLDING Ella on my lap, reading her a story. She leans back against me, and I kiss her on the head, breathing in the lilac scent of her shampoo.

"Read it again, Mommy," she says.

I flip the book back to the beginning.

"Once upon a time—"

Wednesday, January 10, 3:02 a.m., New York

I wake up with a terrible pain in my stomach. The room feels like it's spinning. *No, not again.* But then I nearly begin to laugh with relief. It's okay. I am a full nine months along; this baby is supposed to be arriving. I feel the bed to see if my water has broken, but the sheets are dry. Still, I know the baby is on its way.

"Steve," I say, giggling with excitement, "I'm having a contraction."

Steve's eyes snap open, and he sits up in bed, fast. "I'll call the midwife," he says.

I feel immensely grateful that this pregnancy has been so easy, and I am grateful that I finally have a chance to deliver a baby the way I always wanted: naturally. Obviously, I am eternally thankful that I had access to a good hospital when Ella was born. Now, though, I hope to stay as far away from the hospital as possible. I am having this baby here: at home with Steve. The contraction stops and I breathe a sigh of relief.

Wednesday, January 10, 12:05 p.m., Sacramento

"Mommy, wake up!" Ella says, lifting my eyelid with her little fingers.

Oh, dear. I have to figure out what to do with Ella; there is no way I'll be able to stay asleep in New York while I give birth.

"Baby, Mommy needs to go to bed early. She's really tired. Can you watch Curious George until Daddy gets home?"

Ella nods.

I call Steve at work. "Honey, I'm having the baby in New York. I'm going to be out of commission here for a while. Can you come home?"

"On my way," he says. "And good luck, Angie."

"Thanks."

I practically run upstairs and get into bed.

Wednesday, January 10, 3:10 a.m., New York

I awaken in New York to Steve stroking my forehead.

"You took a little nap, Ang," he says.

"Yeah, well, I had to deal with some stuff in California," I say.

"I talked to Barb. She says to labor on your own for a few hours and then call her when you feel you need her, and she'll come right over. I also ran you a bath."

"Thanks, Steve. You're the best."

Over the next several hours, the labor goes smoothly. Steve lowers the lights and plays the ocean-music CD I got from my Bradley Method instructor. I take warm baths, I use the bathroom, I pace the room, and I kneel over a birthing ball. The contractions are painful, but I breathe through them and find myself still able to talk and joke with Steve. I even eat snacks and drink coconut water.

But then, around noon, everything changes. The contractions get much stronger and much closer together. They also get much more painful. Suddenly, I don't feel quite so in control.

"Call Barb," I say through gritted teeth.

Within ten minutes, our midwife, Barbara, has arrived. She has brought with her a bagful of gear. Her brown, curly hair is streaked with gray, and she projects an aura of calm…calm that I wish I had.

"Barb," I say, reaching out to her. And I immediately start to cry. "It hurts so bad. I can't do this anymore. I need medication. I need to go to the hospital. I thought I could do it, but I can't."

Barb takes my hand. "Angela, you *can* do this. I know it hurts, I know it's hard, but women have been doing this since the beginning of time, and you can do it too. You are doing it."

I nod, my lip quivering. "I'm just so scared."

"Let me examine you," Barb says.

Afterward, she tells me that I am doing great and that I will be ready to start pushing any minute.

"It's too late to go to the hospital now, anyway," she says. "This baby is on its way."

When I feel the need to push, I squat on the floor, Steve holding me in a bear hug from behind. I squeeze his arms and push. The pain is unbearable. I feel as if I am being stretched in half.

"Push through the pain," Barb says.

For half an hour, I push and rest, push and rest. Finally, the baby is crowning.

"Relax. Don't push—just let it come out," Barb says.

I feel a burning like I've never experienced in my life—the "ring of fire" they talked about in my class. And then the baby nearly flies out of me and into Barb's arms.

Barb hands the bloody, squalling, misshapen infant into my arms. Tears pour from my eyes as I clutch the baby to my chest. Our baby. She is perfect. Like Ella. But also not like Ella, her hair darker and thicker.

"I love you," I say. "I loved you before I met you."

Chapter 48

Wednesday, July 4, 11:58 a.m., Sacramento

STEVE, ELLA, AND I are in the car on the way to Steve's parents' house for the day. Steve started his new job and has been working much less than before, eating dinner with the family, and doing a lot of his work at home. Ella seems well adjusted and happy. Steve and I are even thinking about trying for another baby. And finally, I am happy in both of my lives. Most people have enough trouble being happy in one.

Ella counts out loud from her car seat behind us. "One, two, three, four, five, six, seven, eight, nine, ten…"

Steve pats my knee and smiles at Ella in the rearview mirror. "Good job, El. You are a great counter."

"Onze, duex, treize, quatorz, quinz, seize, dix-sept, dix-huit, dix-neuf, vin."

I turn around and look at Ella, shocked to hear her counting in French. I guess my daughter really is smarter than the average child.

"Where did you learn to count in French, Ella? Did they teach you at preschool?"

"Non, Maman, tu m'a donne au Paris."

You taught me in Paris. I feel chills run up my spine.

"What do you mean, honey?" I say. "We've never been to Paris. Please answer Mommy in English."

"You know, Mommy. When we go to sleep, then we live in Paris, and you and Daddy are teaching me French."

I shoot Steve a look, and he massages his temples.

"Ella, you mean, when you go to sleep, you wake up in Paris every time?" he asks her.

"Yeah," Ella says. "We all do!"

I swallow, terrified, yet at the same time grateful that Ella has me to guide her, that while the world may shame and shun her, she has a family that will always believe in her. In fact, she has two families that will always believe in her.

"That's right, Ella. Some people are extra lucky, like you and me and Daddy. We get to have more than one life at the same time."

She grins. "Je vous aime!"

"And we love you too, Ella," I say.

I look out the window, up at the sky, and I feel at peace. I know that somehow, somewhere, my dad is watching over me, making sure I'm okay. And I know that, no matter what, I am blessed because I have found a love greater than any I could ever imagine. A love so great that it exists in multiple realities. Even realities I don't know about, that I only have access to through my daughter. I wonder how many of me there are, how many are driving this same road, how many Ellas, how many Steves. But I know that in the end, it doesn't really matter. I will be content with my two lives, as others are with one, and know that for all the heartbreak I may experience, the joy will overpower it.

About the Author

Jennifer Provenza is an actor, playwright, and professor of theater. She has her BFA from NYU and her MFA from Brooklyn College. Her plays have been performed at NYU, Barnyard Theatre, The Strawberry One-Act Festival, and Gone in 60 in Brooklyn and in Leeds, England. She lives in Sacramento with her husband, two daughters, and their fluffy black cat, Mrs. Sparkles. To learn more, visit her website at www.jenniferprovenza.com.

Made in the USA
San Bernardino, CA
06 January 2017